Praise for CHENDELL: A Natural Warrior

"Chendell starts as a boy-meets-girl story, connecting a girl from the U.S. to a boy in China, told in an unusual, compelling format. It is about love and family, but also about insects and trees. When boy and girl become a supercouple, the reader accompanies them on a wild, dangerous journey, and then, when your heart is in your throat, something happens that is shocking, unique and utterly heartwarming. Leslie Landis has written a tale I'll never forget. Bravo!"

— Thom Racina
Emmy nominated writer and author of *Snow Angel*

"Leslie Landis takes us on an incredible trip with CHENDELL. A superhero story packed with a delightful page turning packet of ingredients—adventure, love plus great humor and wit. CHENDELL and its heroes are just begging to be given the big screen treatment."

— Ivor Davis, author of *"The Beatles and Me On Tour"*
and *"Ladies and Gentlemen...The Penguins!"*

"I love sharing books like CHENDELL that inspire us to reach soul deep and inspire us to become better human beings... that help us believe in magic and the power of Mother Nature."

@waterthruskin

D1367119

CHENDELL
A NATURAL WARRIOR

LESLIE I. LANDIS

JÖL

A CHENDELL™ ADVENTURE

WGA 1931511

Published by Waldo LLC

First edition, 2019

Library of Congress Cataloging-in-Publication Data
Landis, Leslie I.
   Chendell: A Natural Warrior / Leslie Landis. First Edition.
ISBN 978-1-7329114-0-6 (pbk.)
I. Title. II. Title: A Natural Warrior. III. Title: Chendell.

Cover and interior illustrations by Naomi Alessandra
Designed by Naomi Alessandra and Randi Karabin

www.chendell.com

To Martin,

When you found me, I found myself.
Always, with love.

"The only thing that is constant is change."
—Heraclitus of Ephesus, 500 BC

CONTENTS

FORESHADOW

We were deeper into the rainforest than we had ever been. The heat was stifling. The forest floor was often muddy and slippery. It was difficult to stay on our feet. My instinct was to reach for vines and tree trunks but that was risky. In shades of gray and black gloom—I didn't always know what I was grasping. Was it a vine or a snake hanging from a tree?

Sweat was pouring off all of us. The darkness was oppressive. And when a rare ray of light did penetrate to the forest floor, the glare was blinding. The constant shrieking of birds added to my anxiety. I had to remind myself why we were here. We were searching for healing discoveries. But why here? What were we thinking? This area was dangerous. Full of natural risks. It felt as if the forest was our enemy. But I was wrong. The real enemy walked on two legs.

1

THE TREE AND ME

Guilin, China

In a rural hamlet near Guilin, China, lived the Chen family. The father, Huiliang, was a fifth-generation farmer. The mother, Ling, was a respected herbalist. Their one child, a son, was Jinsong. Jinsong and those closest to him tell his story.

JINSONG

My earliest memory is of the pine tree in the front courtyard of our house. It was a Chinese Red Pine. A common tree in central and southern China. A pretty tree with a wide rounded crown and long needles on lengthy branches. It had a soft fluffy look. And though it was far from full grown when I was a young boy, it still provided cool shade as it towered over our small one-story farmhouse.

I think it was my first memory but maybe it just seems that way because my mother told me nearly every day how I was named after this tree. "Jinsong, your name means sturdy pine. I gave you this name so you would be like the pine in our courtyard. Strong and straight and tall."

Was that why in my young dreamy mind I believed the tree and I were related? That the tree and I could talk to each other? Even think the same thoughts? A childish fantasy? No. Not really.

HUILIANG (Father)

I was happy Jinsong was the kind of boy who wanted to learn from me. We had a close father-son bond. And Jinsong was a strong boy who willingly helped me plant and harvest in the rice paddies. Not like many of the other boys of his generation who only thought of themselves and of having fun. Little Emperors we called them because, as the only child, their parents indulged them.

We talked a lot but our conversations were mainly the "how to do" kind of things. How to plant rice, how to fix farm equipment, how to harvest, how to fish. Other things I tried to teach by example. How to treat others, how to value your wife and especially how to appreciate the earth.

JINSONG

I did grow strong and straight and tall but I doubt my name had anything to do with my strength. It was likely the farm work. When I wasn't in school I worked with Father. I loved being with him. And my contributing efforts made me feel important and worthwhile.

We planted rice shoots in the watery, soft ground. Watching them grow was magical. As they reached toward the sky with the sure potential of young living things—I felt their energy. I heard them communicating with each other. And I could "talk" to them. Though our valley was ideal for growing rice and all the farmers did well, Father's crop was always the best with the most abundant and thickest grains. I urged the rice plants to grow. To make the most of their fleeting lives. They knew and accepted their fate because they had purpose. No life is too short or wasted if it is lived with purpose. But when Father and I pulled the plants out of the ground—I heard their pain. I soothed this transition by reminding them of their important role. Feeding the hungry people of China.

Sometimes when Father wasn't farming he took me fishing at the wide, slow-moving Li River not far from our house. It was a special time. Watching rafts being poled down the river. Seeing fishermen use cormorant birds to catch fish. But the best part was spending time with Father. Baiting the hook for his pole and mine. Talking. Pulling the fish in together. He would teach me how to do something but then let me do it myself. Father never criticized me or made me feel incompetent if I made a mistake. He would patiently show me again. He was just like the meaning of his name. Kind and good.

HUILIANG (Father)

I had become a farmer because my father was a farmer and his father and his father. I liked farming. I liked seeing the tender rice plants grow. I liked knowing their growth was the result of my hard work.

Our farm was in the Dragon's Backbone. A truly spectacular long, deep valley with terraced rice paddies reaching as high as its steep sides. It would be difficult to live in this area without an appreciation of the beauty of nature. My family has always lived in this special place.

We had seen hard times but at least our farm provided enough to eat. And because we were peasants, we did not suffer during the Cultural Revolution. My family kept their heads down and tended to business. Sometimes that meant attending a rally in town to hold up my Little Red Book as I shouted Mao's name. Of course, as a boy I was very patriotic. I believed Mao was a god given to China. Lucky China. But after Mao's death, things changed. We became more aware of the world outside our country. Maybe China had not been so lucky.

JINSONG

My mother was more critical. For good reason. I was messy and clumsy and she blamed my inattention on my daydreaming. "Jinsong, you are always leaving things behind, dropping things, breaking things and bumping into things. The pine tree drops fewer needles than everything you drop. Stop daydreaming and pay attention!"

What did I daydream about? The usual things boys find interesting. Being strong, being good at sports, being successful. And being popular with girls. But girls were a great mystery to me. I didn't understand them. What were they giggling about? What did they like in a boy? Obviously my mother was a girl but that didn't help me understand the rest of them. I hoped that one day a girl would find me interesting and even attractive. And maybe I would have as happy a marriage as my parents had.

LING (Mother)

Like the pine tree we named him after, Jinsong was strong and straight and eventually tall. Also like the tree, every wind made him bend this way and that way. He was easily distracted and always daydreaming.

Jinsong was born on the ninth day of the ninth month. The lucky number nine is the dragon's number. But when he was little I thought he was more like a dragonfly than a dragon. Always flitting from one fantasy to another.

Yet he was inquisitive. I was pleased that, as he got older, he took an interest in my herbal healing. Whenever he could, he came with me to find the plants I needed. He liked learning about which ones were good for different health problems. His interest in healing made me think he might be a doctor if he would concentrate on his studies. And if we could afford to pay for a university education.

But he was shy around girls. I worried he would never marry. And the number of boys in our village far outnumbered the girls. I believed he would have to go away to find a wife. I just didn't realize how far that journey would take him.

JINSONG

I did pay close attention to one thing my mother did. She was an herbalist. She learned it from her mother who learned it from her mother and on and on from ancestor to ancestor.

Mother would take me with her to find special plants, mushrooms and herbs for healing powders and tonics. I liked going into the woods and learning the names of the different plants. Which ones were useful and which ones to avoid. Sometimes when our search was unproductive, I asked the surrounding trees and vegetation where we could find a specific plant or fungus. Then I led Mother to the indicated location. She was always surprised when we "suddenly" came upon the plant she sought. She called me her lucky charm.

I didn't consider it unusual for Mother to be teaching me about medicinal plants. Since she didn't have a daughter, who else was she going to share this knowledge with? I once asked her if she wished I had been a girl. Mother said no but her face was sad. Many years later I realized she had wanted a son—and a daughter. But parents were only allowed one child so she had to be satisfied with me.

On one of our plant-gathering trips I questioned why she only used plants to heal. Why not use animal parts—a bear's liver or a tiger's bone or an elephant's tusk—as other healers did? Mother laughed and explained. "Those things don't work. They have no curing power. People are killing animals for nothing. And as for an elephant's tusk, you might as well use your fingernail clippings. Same thing. No, Jinsong, I will stick to plants. They give us everything we need. They are the true healers."

LING (Mother)

I married young. Only 16 years old. I wanted to study more but in those days families had more than one child. I was the middle child of five—two older brothers and two younger sisters. Eating came first and the boys' education was second.

My marrying young was my parents' solution to having too many mouths to feed and not enough money. But when I met Huiliang, I knew he was a good man and I wanted to be with him. It didn't hurt that he was handsome.

Soon after we were married I became pregnant with Jinsong. What a blessing to have a son. And about a year after his birth, I became pregnant again. Since we were allowed only one child, I tried to hide my pregnancy. But I was thin and I showed early. I well remember the day I got a visit from our village's Party member. My heart was beating fast. I knew what it meant. My tears had no effect. She took me to a hospital to have my pregnancy ended.

When Huiliang learned from a neighbor where I was, he rushed to the hospital. He could do nothing to stop the procedure. But when he learned that they were also going to sterilize me, he talked them into giving him a vasectomy instead. He didn't want me to experience a double loss. My love. My Huiliang.

🍃　🍃　🍃

HUILIANG (Father)
Ling and I always stressed to Jinsong that school came first. We made a plan for him when he was born. In the new China, we saw that he could have a future other than farming. Farming is honorable work but it was also hard work and provided a meager living. New prospects were becoming available to the young. We wanted Jinsong to have those opportunities. This was our dream for him. And we were willing to do anything we could to make it come true.

But we did not know how we would finance his education beyond secondary school. That is why I encouraged my wife's idea of using her excellent knowledge of herbs to make and sell beauty creams. And as her business grew, I unofficially leased our farm and farmhouse to my brother. I was happy to work with Ling. I married a smart woman. Luck was with me.

LING (Mother)

Every mother has dreams for her child and wants the best for him. I was no different. I wanted Jinsong to become a professional. But we didn't have the money for his education beyond secondary school. Though I added to the family income with my herbal sales, it wasn't enough to pay for university.

Chinese women have always been careful to cover their faces and their arms when they worked outside. I certainly did when I helped Huiliang farm. I did not like farm labor. Too hard. Too dirty. Too hot. In modern times most young women felt the same. Instead of farm work they chose to go to the cities and work in factories and in offices. But from the ads I saw in magazines and newspapers, I realized they still cared about their skin. I decided to use my knowledge of plants to make my own skin care products. My business grew and grew. It was successful. We finally had the money needed for Jinsong's education. Our son would become a professional. And if we needed his aid when we were old, he would be able to help us.

JINSONG

Mother was clever and intelligent. Just like the meaning of her name. She made extra money by selling her medicinal herbs in the nearby village. But before I started secondary school, she began using her knowledge of plants to make creams and lotions. Beauty products. These became very popular with the women in our area so she hired women in neighboring towns and villages to sell her beauty products—Chen's Transformation Youth-Preserving Creams. As the demand increased, she could not keep up with the orders.

Since most rural land is collectively owned in China, Father informally leased his land to his brother Zihao and began working with Mother. And when the sales outpaced what the two of them could produce, they found a factory that would make her products to her specifications. They quickly branched out to the province, to the adjacent region and then to the country. I was amazed by their entrepreneurship. By their initiative.

But what I didn't realize then was that my parents had a goal. They had a plan for me and it wasn't being a farmer. My father was going to be the last Chen of his line to farm. I was going to Beijing. I was going to university.

🍃　　🍃　　🍃

LING (Mother)
A lot changed when Jinsong was 14. He started secondary school and we moved from our simple 600-square-foot, one-story brick farmhouse. Over the years, Huiliang had divided the space into two small bedrooms and a main room. He covered the dirt floor with wood planks. I decorated it with embroidered quilts and pillows. A small shrine was set up to honor our ancestors. The kitchen was a "wall kitchen." A

little cubicle with a window. No indoor plumbing. Five other farmhouses were grouped near ours. Sort of a mini-village. Living there was perfectly fine for us. It was home.

JINSONG
With the success of Mother's business, my parents built a new house in Guilin—the biggest nearby city. Guilin is in a beautiful area noted for its conical-shaped mountains. These are shown in paintings that often hang in many Chinese restaurants in the United States.

The new house was much bigger and made of cement with a green tile roof. It had three floors and modern conveniences. Kitchens with the latest appliances and indoor toilets on every floor. Polished tile floors in the common areas and beautiful wood floors in the bedrooms. And we had a television.

Even with all these luxuries, Father had a difficult time persuading Mother to move. I think that she was superstitious about leaving our old house because of the pine tree. And though she denied it, I knew she felt the tree was good luck. Probably because I was named after it and our life had been good there. But since our old house and farm would remain in the family, Father was finally able to convince her. He told her, "If things don't work out, we can always return."

HUILIANG (Father)
The new house was better for the business. The first floor was used as an office and we lived on the spacious second floor. One of Mother's sisters, Mei, and her family lived on the top floor.

Mei and four other women worked for us. They placed orders for supplies, coordinated the production of the beauty products and filled orders. Everyone worked at a big wooden table in the middle of the ground floor main room.

LING (Mother)

The idea of building a new house was exciting. And it made sense to move to Guilin. We needed to be in the city to better manage our growing business. Also, Jinsong would be able to go to a superior school. But as the time neared to move, I became hesitant. Our life in our little farmhouse had been good. We didn't live in luxury but we lived in happiness. And our pine tree—the tree Jinsong was named after—had brought us luck. Would we leave our good fortune behind us? But finally, as Huiliang said, I had to put Jinsong's education and the business ahead of my fears.

The new house had a long, rectangular wood table. And on that sizable table I placed a large, bright yellow porcelain bowl. It was decorated in the Qing Dynasty style with a large green dragon on each side. I filled it with the pine cones I had gathered from the pine tree at our old house. It was my way of bringing our good luck with us.

JINSONG

A strange thing happened as we were moving from our farmhouse. I heard the pine tree communicating with the other trees. It said, "He is leaving me. I don't want him to go. We have grown tall and straight and strong together." Though hearing these thoughts affected me deeply, I didn't tell my parents. I feared they would think I was hallucinating. But after our move, I never missed a trip back to the farm to see Uncle and his family. And every time, I heard the pine tree say, "Aaaah, he is back. It is good to feel his presence, his positive energy. And we are both taller now." I actually heard this. I know I always understood tree "talk" but as I got older, my senses and awareness became more acute.

I left my childhood home and friends. And even though I was then almost 15 and my interests had changed, I still missed the land and the woods and the sense of freedom. I was happy exploring the natural world.

But there were benefits to being in town. I could attend a very good senior secondary school. One that offered better preparation for university. And I made good friends at my new school. Three guys who were also focused on continuing their studies after graduation. They were Liang, Bai and Jiang. Jiang and I formed an especially close bond. We both wanted to become doctors and eventually complete our education in America. Liang planned on becoming a structural engineer. Bai wanted to be a computer programmer.

English was the foreign language we studied in secondary school. Our instructor, Mr. Ashley Pardue, was from America. From the city of Mobile in a state called Alabama. To this day my English is slightly accented with a southern drawl.

He gave us English names to use in class. I became "Jim" since he thought it was close to Jin, as in Jinsong. I liked it because it was short and easy to pronounce. Jiang was called "Jack." Mr. Pardue wanted to call Liang "Lee" but he objected because Lee is such a common Chinese familial name. Instead Liang became "Lance." Mr. Pardue said Bai had hair like David Bowie so his name was "Bowie." Bai was thrilled with the association and his English name.

ASHLEY PARDUE (English teacher)

I couldn't believe it! Twenty-one years old and there I was in Guilin, China. A beautiful city in a beautiful area. Teaching great kids English. I had taken standard Chinese, Mandarin, at the University of Alabama and this opportunity gave me a chance to become proficient in the language. I hoped that when I returned to the U.S., I would get a job with a corporation that needed someone fluent in Mandarin. Meanwhile, I was having a great experience.

The kids I taught were not much younger than me. I could relate to them. There was a group of guys who called themselves the Fearsome Four. I liked them. Especially one of the guys. Jinsong. For a teenager, he was open to new ideas, different experiences and meeting new people. We had many interesting conversations.

I gave him the English name of Jim because it was similar to Jinsong. But then I started to call him "James," the formal version of Jim. Somehow Jim was too "everyday" for such an impressive young man. I explained to him that James was a common name. But since Americans liked to make names informal and casual, James sometimes became Jamie. And Jamie was a gender-neutral name like my name, Ashley. It could be the name of a boy or a girl. He liked that idea. He said it was becoming more popular in modern China for families to use feminine characters in boys' names and vice versa. "Jamie," he said, "felt modern and friendly."

JINSONG

We all studied hard since we would eventually take an exam that would determine if we could go to a good university. But when we weren't studying, we played soccer and basketball. And, of course, we looked for girls. While my friends easily talked to girls and spent time with them, I felt shy and uncomfortable. That changed with Lijuan.

JIANG (best friend)

We studied a lot. But we four—the Fearsome Four as we called ourselves in English—also had fun. We did stupid things like taking a piglet out of a farmer's yard and putting it in an adjoining yard. Then we would hide and watch as the two farmers argued over the "stolen pig." Or we'd catch a fish and sneak it into a woman's market shopping bag just to watch her shocked surprise. We wanted to see who would complain to the clerk that they didn't buy the fish and who would gleefully run home with it.

Jinsong and I took Shaolin Kung Fu lessons together. We were the best ones at our martial arts academy. We challenged each other all the time. Then Jinsong started practicing very hard and he won more than I did. Maybe he was a little better than me but not a lot better.

And we rode our bikes around town looking for girls. When we saw a group—and they always seemed to be in groups—we would race to see who would get to them first. We told each other the fastest guy there got first pick. Of course, that was just in our minds. The girls had their own ideas about who they were interested in. We told Jinsong not to take the lead because he never knew what to say. But he was strong and fast. And he liked to outrace us. When he got to the girls, he became a statue until someone else arrived and started the conversation. Then a miracle happened. He got a girlfriend. Her name was Lijuan. And she actually "got" him.

LIJUAN (girlfriend)
I immediately liked Jinsong. He was good looking and tall and smart. He had thick black hair and the darkest brown eyes. He had such a penetrating look. Sometimes I felt he could see right through me. I thought he looked like a Chinese version of David Beckham and I looked like Victoria Beckham. We were perfect for each other.

But Jinsong was shy. He wouldn't or couldn't talk to me. I decided that it was up to me to make the first move before another girl did. So when he and his friends bicycled up to us—my girlfriends and me—I jumped in front of his bike and fell down. It makes me laugh now when I remember the shocked look on his face. His bike just brushed me. I wasn't hurt. But Jinsong didn't know that. He felt terrible. As he helped me up, he asked, "Are you okay?" I said my leg hurt and suggested he give me a ride home.

There I was sitting on the center crossbar of his bike with his arms hugging me as he held the handlebars. We were so close that I hoped he couldn't feel how fast my heart was beating. When we got to my house, I invited him in. I made my favorite tea, Lushan Yunwu. Jinsong said it was also his favorite tea. I think the tea helped him relax. We talked about school, about his friends and family, about our plans for the future. Before he left I said, "Okay, we'll go to a movie tomorrow." Poor boy. He thought it was his idea. But I didn't feel guilty. Jinsong needed a girlfriend. He needed me.

We started to spend time together. Conversation came easily. He learned girls were not strange or different. However, what was not obvious to Jinsong was clear to all our friends. And everyone teased him about how I "got" him. We didn't care. The important thing was that we really liked each other. We enjoyed being together.

I admit that I fantasized about us getting married one day. But deep down I knew that wasn't going to happen. I knew Jinsong's family had plans and the money to send him to university. I knew he wanted to study in the United States after that. I also knew that I didn't want to wait that long to get married. And I had plans of my own. After graduation from secondary school, I was going to Hangzhou to get a factory job. I wanted to be in a big coastal city and help my family financially.

🍃 🍃 🍃

HUILIANG (Father)
Everything was going well for us. The business was prospering and so was Jinsong. Guilin offered him new opportunities, activities and friends. The move to the city had been a good decision. Then I began to feel tired, listless, achy. I thought it was due to getting older. Or my body was worn out from farm work. Finally I went to a doctor. Too late.

I wrote my thoughts down. I wanted Jinsong to know my feelings. And remember me. I would have liked to travel. To see more of the world. That was impossible. I was married at 20 and a father at 21. But now my son will be educated. He will be able to take the journeys I could not. Would not. Yes, I regret not having traveled. But I did go to Shanghai once. I regret the daughter that Ling and I might have had. But I have a wonderful son and I am proud of him. I cannot share in Jinsong's future. Will luck shine on him? Will he find a good and loving wife as I did? Where will his travels take him? What will he become? I will not live to know the answers. Still I can say at the end of my days I have had a good life. A happy life. How many people can say that?

JINSONG
When I was almost finished with secondary school, the worst thing happened. Father was diagnosed with pancreatic cancer. Mother and I were beyond upset and frightened. We cried and cried. Only Father was calm. Of course Mother tried the herbal remedies she hoped would work.

LING (Mother)
Besides my herbal medicines, I insisted Huiliang try Western medicine. But the doctors said the cancer had spread beyond being treatable. Huiliang was calm. He knew. He was prepared for the inevitable. He had not been feeling well for a long time but he kept it to himself. He was like many men who don't want to go to a doctor to find out how sick they are. Six months later, he died.

JINSONG

Father's diagnosis and the suddenness of his death was a shock to me. I couldn't understand why there was nothing that could have been done. And I was mad at Mother. Why couldn't she help him? Why couldn't she cure him with her herbs? With tears, she sadly responded to my angry blaming, "Maybe there is another plant in the world that could have saved him but I only have the plants in China."

Mother cried, "I knew it was a mistake to move. To leave our farmhouse. To leave our beautiful pine tree. We left our good luck behind." Father's death made me fear she might be right. I still didn't tell her about the pine tree communicating its thoughts to me. If she believed me, it would only make her feel worse about our moving away.

LING (Mother)

Jinsong had been taking Shaolin Kung Fu since middle school. It was good discipline for his mind and body. But he did not take his lessons seriously until Huiliang became ill and died. Then he practiced all the time. I realized this was a way for him to free his anger and grief. And to focus his energy in a positive direction. He became very good at kung fu. However, he felt guilty about going away to university and leaving me alone.

JINSONG

After Father died I didn't want to go away to university. I wanted to help Mother in her business as Father had done. But she said the reason they—she and Father—had worked was the start of his journey. How far would it take him? How far away from me? It is a parent's mission to prepare their child for the outside world. It is a parent's pain to see them go. Yet this was why his father and I had worked hard. A successful future for Jinsong was our goal. A happy life for him was our hope. We Chinese believe in luck but I also believe a person makes their own luck. Jinsong's education would bring him luck.

WENDY (Mrs. Kindle)

Jamie became family. When he was home and available, he ate with us and we included him in our family activities. The zoo, the aquarium, the park, the swimming pool. Things like that. And he played with the kids. Hide and seek, painting, board games. He taught them kung fu moves too. I was delighted and amused by how seriously they took their martial arts "training." But sometimes I got the feeling that Dongmei resented Jamie or maybe she resented his relationship with the children.

DONGMEI (housekeeper)

Jinsong was okay but the children were too excited when they were with him. Then I was the one who had to calm them down.

🍃 🍃 🍃

JINSONG (JAMIE)

The Kindles had a pet dog. That was something else I hadn't experienced. While I was growing up, we had farm animals. A water buffalo, chickens, ducks. And we had a couple of cats to keep the mouse population under control. I always liked animals but we didn't keep them as pets. And though we never had a dog, we also never saw them as a meal. Mother thought that was an old-fashioned practice. And she was aware that dogs were considered worthy companions in most of the world. Even in China—especially in the cities—it was becoming popular to a have a pet dog.

The Kindle dog was named Bao Wao. They thought his name was funny because it sounded like "bow-wow" in English. They told me that was how young English-speaking children think a dog's bark sounds. They got the "bao" part right because it sounds similar to "bow," which means precious. But "wao" is just made up. Anyway, Chinese children say "wang-wang" for a dog's bark.

Bao Wao was a pug. An odd-looking little dog with a round body, short legs, a flat face and bulging eyes. I didn't know this breed originated in China. The Kindle children had a lot of fun playing with him. And I learned to play with him. Throwing a ball for him. Playing tug-of-war. Rubbing his tummy. I even taught him a trick. Shaking hands. I grew to like him a lot.

WENDY (Mrs. Kindle)

I was particularly interested in animal welfare. I shared with Jamie a lot of material about how people abuse animals. I know my passion was obvious when I talked about how elephants and rhinoceros were being hunted to extinction just for their horns and tusks.

JINSONG (JAMIE)

I remembered Mother's disbelief that people thought animal parts had special healing powers. I was excited when an online search found Chinese organizations working to protect animals. One was the Chinese Animal Protection Network. And another one was Chinese Companion Animal Protection Network. I joined them both. I participated in online signing events and distributed educational literature. I also made contributions.

WENDY (Mrs. Kindle)

Thank goodness Jamie was home. Thank goodness he saved Bao Wao. Thank goodness this exceptional young man rented a room in our house. As he liked to say, "Luck was with us."

JINSONG (JAMIE)

Leung Wen's story had a footnote. The Kindles sort of adopted the Leung family. They would bring them food. They gave Mingzhu a computer so she could take online courses. Wendy also got Mingzhu a wheelchair and had a ramp built. She was finally able to easily get out of their one-room basement apartment. Wendy said, "To whom much is given, much is expected."

WEN (reformed dog-snatcher)

It was a mystery to me how good could come from the bad I had done. The Kindles could have hated me but instead they were kind to me and my family. Because of them I worked harder in school. I made new friends. Honorable friends. And I made my goal to someday take care of my family. Meanwhile, NianNian brought a lot of joy to my sister. Really, to all of us.

🍃 🍃 🍃

JINSONG (JAMIE)

After finishing university in three and a half years, I applied to and was accepted by the University of California, Davis. I felt excited but also guilty and anxious about being even farther away from Mother. I decided to spend the extra semester and summer with her before leaving for the United States.

It was sad to say goodbye to the Kindles. Especially the kids. I had grown close to them. They were my little brothers and sister. As I hugged them goodbye, they cried. And I couldn't hide my tears. But I knew we would see each other again. Either in China or in the U.S.

When I had the extended time at home with Mother, I decided to tell her about my communicating with trees. I didn't want to go away with this secret between us. Even if she thought I was crazy, I knew she would still love me. But what surprised me was that she wasn't surprised.

LING (Mother)

I was glad Jinsong confided in me. I had suspected for a long time that he could communicate with trees and plants. I would see him listening intently while he sat under our pine tree. And the strange ability he had to locate herbs I was looking for. And the way Huiliang's rice plants grew tall and full when Jinsong worked with him. Another parent might think her child was delusional but occasionally I heard trees and plants "talking." When that happened, I was able to find the best medicines to help people.

I explained, "If plants can grow, can reproduce, can register sensations and shock and fear, why couldn't they and why wouldn't they communicate with one another? And with us? Plants are as alive as you and me."

JINSONG

Mother was more sophisticated and self-educated than I realized. "There is wisdom," she said, "to be gained from your special ability. Use it to further your work." I then realized that Mother's fear of moving from our farmhouse wasn't just about luck. She didn't want to leave an old friend. The pine tree.

Mother also surprised me by how independent she had become. She was occupied with her business. She now had 15 people working in our house. They didn't all fit around her big table. Some were stuck at little desks in every corner. So she was making plans to move the office to a bigger space in an office building.

LING (Mother)
Besides working hard, I had a group of about ten friends. Both men and women. We took trips together. I felt more comfortable traveling with others. We had gone to places in China. Shanghai and Xian to see the terracotta warriors. And to Thailand. My group wanted to go to the United States next. But at my request, they decided to wait until Jinsong was settled in school there.

JINSONG (JAMIE)
Mother was busy. We didn't spend as much time together as I anticipated. But I had a good time at home. I renewed my closeness with Jiang. He had changed. Had grown. And was in a serious relationship. His girlfriend, Chunhua, and I got along well. She was easygoing and patient. Perfect for Jiang.

CHUNHUA (Jiang's girlfriend)
I finally got to meet Jinsong. Jiang talked about him all the time. He was nice. Very likable. And handsome too. The three of us went to the new "hot" spots in Guilin. Bars and dance

clubs. And sometimes I made it a double date by including one of my girlfriends.

JINSONG (JAMIE)

I had fun. I was more relaxed than I had been in a long time. I almost forgot my concerns about going to school in a different and unfamiliar country. Was my English good enough for technical courses? Would I achieve my goal in medicinal botany? I was certainly excited to have new experiences and meet new people. But I also felt an underlying uneasiness about this new chapter in my life. I pushed my worries away. After all, I thought, feeling some apprehension was probably normal.

When I heard Lijuan was home on a short vacation from her job in Hangzhou, I went to see her. She seemed worldly. Dressed in the latest styles. At first she didn't like her factory job. But she stuck with it and was promoted to a supervisor position. Now she was earning more money. And she enjoyed telling people what to do. I remembered how Lijuan liked to be in charge. That was one way she hadn't changed. Lijuan had a boyfriend in Hangzhou. They were planning to get married. "He is better looking than you, Jinsong," she said. We both laughed. I was happy for her.

Too soon it was late August. I made a last visit to the pine tree at our farm house. I told it I wouldn't be back for a long time. The tree expressed regret, "I'm sorry you are leaving but one day you will help trees live a safer life." With no more explanation, this prediction was intriguing and unsettling. After all, I was planning on a career in cancer research. How did that relate to trees? Even so, I was moved by the pine tree's prophecy. I hugged it. With emotion I said, "I will miss you." Then it spoke once more, "The day will come when we are together again."

LING (Mother)

I saw Jinsong off on a flight to Hong Kong. He planned on sightseeing there for a few days before his flight to San Francisco. Then more exploring there before his bus ride to the University of California, Davis. I made him his favorite treat for the trip. Almond cookies. And we made plans for his visit home during winter break. We would also be together when my touring companions and I traveled to San Francisco in the spring.

He was my baby and now he was going out into a big world. All the way to America. But we had a bond that would never be broken. He would always be my boy. I made a life for myself so he could have his own life. I had heard this saying: "If you want them to come back, you have to let them go." I hid my tears as I sent him off. I had a feeling—and my feelings were true—that he would do great things. He had the special gift of hearing plants. He would take that gift further than I had. He would make a difference in the world.

3
—

THE BUGS AND ME

Vermont, United States

In a suburb of Burlington, Vermont, lived the Dell family. The father, Robert, was a well-regarded university professor of electrical engineering and a part-time inventor. The mother, Margaret, was a respected retired family court judge. They had two children, Harris and Robin. Robin and those closest to her tell her story.

ROBIN

I remember thinking at an early age that we were the perfect family. A mom and dad and two kids—a boy and girl. My dad, Robert, was called Bobby. My mom, Margaret, was called Maggie. Harris—four years older than me—was Harry. Everyone called me Robbie. The only one in our family who didn't have a nickname was our dog Waldo.

Harry was named after Dad's brother, Harris, who died at 21 from leukemia. Most people thought I was named after the bird. But I was named after Dad. And I have one of those gender-neutral names. Usually a boy's spelling is "Robin" and a girl's is "Robyn." Apparently, my parents didn't know that.

Except for the winter weather, we lived in a perfect place. Sherburne, Vermont. It's a beautiful suburb of the biggest city in Vermont, Burlington, with a population of 43,000. Not really that big. Sherburne had only 7,000 people and felt more rural than suburban. Many houses are on several acres of rolling land with stands of trees all over. And there's a traditional charming Vermont village at its heart. Lake Champlain is on one side and the Adirondack Mountains can be seen across the lake. The Vermont mountains—the Green Mountains—form a backdrop on the other side. A great place to grow up.

BOBBY (Dad)

Robbie had a problem. She couldn't sit still. She was always running and jumping and climbing. She threw herself into any activity 200 percent. We called her "Wild Girl." But when Robbie was in first grade, it was apparent she was struggling in school. She couldn't stay in her seat and pay attention. She was diagnosed with ADHD. It stands for Attention Deficit Hyperactivity Disorder.

MAGGIE (Mom)

Bobby and I didn't want to use medication. We tried other things. We changed her diet. We cut out all preservatives and food coloring. We tried vitamin supplements. We took her for behavioral therapy. Nothing worked. Then one day Bobby noticed how fascinated Robbie was with the ants marching along our driveway. How she would sit quietly for a long time while watching at them. So he bought her an ant farm.

ROBIN

Dad gave me an ant farm. I loved it! I spent hours watching the ants moving and digging between those panes of glass. Not only did I find their little world absorbing but it calmed me down. I guess it was a form of meditation. And then a strange thing happened. I would just think I wanted the ants to tunnel in a different direction and they would. Or I would pick out one ant to be the leader in a certain tunnel and it became the leader.

When I told my parents about my ability to control the ants, they gave each other sideways glances. They said my ability was wonderful but I should keep it hush-hush. I got the message. Even at that young age, I recognized they were rational people. My thinking I could control ants was irrational. I thought if my parents didn't believe me, no one was going to believe me. And I certainly knew better than to tell Harry—the biggest tease on Earth. From that day on, I always kept my power a secret. Almost always.

BOBBY (Dad)

I'll never forget the day Robbie told us she could control the activity of ants. Of course, Maggie and I didn't want to spoil Robbie's imagination. And we were happy that the ant farm had the effect of calming her down. Of helping her concentrate. We knew she would grow out of this childhood fantasy. So we told her to keep her "unique" ability a secret. I said, "The world isn't ready to accept your special power."

ROBIN

I never lost my interest in ants. But I also became fascinated with bees. I begged my parents for a beehive. Since bees can't live in a "bee farm" and they fly around and sometimes sting, my parents were hesitant. They finally gave in to my pleas.

I loved watching the bees. I loved putting on all the protective gear—until I realized that I didn't need it. I could keep the bees from stinging me. I could think the bees into flying in any direction. When I found out one of our neighbors had sprayed their flowers with a pesticide, I had the bees go somewhere safer for their pollen. I was hooked. I knew from a young age what I wanted to do. I wanted to work with insects.

MAGGIE (Mom)
When Robbie was six, she was diagnosed with ADHD and I was diagnosed with multiple sclerosis. Thank goodness, Robbie's condition greatly improved. Mine, on the other hand, took a relapsing-remitting course. At first my symptoms weren't too bad. Numbness, weakness and tremors in my legs alternated with periods of remission. But overall the disease progressed steadily. And though I used a wheelchair most of the time, I did have good days when I could rely on a cane.

BOBBY (Dad)
When Maggie could no longer climb the stairs to our second-floor master bedroom, we moved from a big house to a bigger house. Four bedrooms with a ground-floor master bedroom, five bathrooms, three fireplaces, 4,300 square feet on over two wooded acres. Newly built in the Dutch Colonial style. Our faux "period" house.

ROBIN

I would describe our old house as rustic modern. Very woodsy.
Yet with contemporary lines, three bedrooms, three and a half
bathrooms, 3,400 square feet on just a little over one acre. A
big house but it felt cozy to me. I loved the big deck where we
could see the lake. And even though it had a family room, I
liked to curl up with a book by the living room stone fireplace.
It was a quiet space where I could concentrate.

My bedroom faced the Green Mountains where Dad took
Harry and me on hikes. We would compete to see who spotted a wild animal first. Dad and Harry always objected to my
idea of including bugs. Animals only. But when I looked at
the mountains from my window, I liked to imagine what the
animals and the insects were doing in their mountain home.
Good thoughts. Good memories.

At our new house, we still had a view of the lake. This time
my bedroom faced it. That was nice. I liked seeing the wind
whip up waves and watching the mists roll off the water. I
missed our old house but this one made life easier for Mom.

That was most important. And the extra bedroom meant Aunt Sue, Mom's sister, didn't have to room with me when she came to visit.

🍃   🍃   🍃

BOBBY (Dad)

As a professor of electrical engineering at the University of Vermont in Burlington, my claim to fame was when I collaborated in developing an armature device to deal with armature flux. We placed another winding in close proximity to the armature winding and had it carry the same current in the opposite direction. That nullified the armature field. I still get a royalty from the device.

ROBIN

Despite Dad's technical expertise—or maybe because of it—he was into jokes. I called him the "Joke Master." He remembered jokes forever and was quick to find a gag for any occasion. I'll give you an example. One time we went to a seafood restaurant and he ordered lobster. When the waiter served him the lobster, Dad asked him why it only had one claw. The waiter said it lost the other claw in a fight. Dad said, "Bring me the winner." Even the waiter cracked up.

Dad also used humor to ease tough situations like Mom's MS. For instance, he liked to sing "Merrily We Roll Along" when he pushed her wheelchair. Maybe humor was his way of dealing with his fear for Mom and what her future held. But truthfully, it helped us all. Especially Mom. He made her laugh. Made us all laugh. Better to laugh than to cry.

BOBBY (Dad)

I was the family activity director. We flew kites, threw boomerangs and shot archery. We went on hikes. And when Maggie's condition deteriorated, sailing continued to be a family activity she could do with us. We just all helped her get into the boat.

We didn't hunt but not because I didn't believe in it. I just didn't think that hunting with a rifle—especially with a scope—was a sport. The animal doesn't stand much of a chance. I feel if someone wants to hunt for amusement, then use a scopeless bow and arrow. Do it the old-fashioned way. Anyway, no one in our family was interested in killing animals.

ROBIN

Mom had a passion for cooking. But when it became too physically difficult for her, Dad became a culinary wizard. I cooked with him. So did Harry when he was home from college. It wasn't a chore. Dad made it fun with hilarious running commentaries on his unusual combinations of food. Whatever he found in the refrigerator. Watermelon and broccoli. Potatoes and yogurt. Green beans cooked in orange juice. Sounds awful but we had a good laugh when his strange mishmashes didn't taste good. And we were often surprised when they were delicious. Now strange combinations are the restaurant rage. Dad was ahead of his time.

HARRY (brother)

When Robbie was born, it was the worst day of my four-year-old life. I begged my parents to take her back to the hospital. But since they didn't, I devoted myself to making her life miserable. I teased her a lot. Threatened to beat her up or drown her in the lake or throw her off the roof. Just seeing me would make her cry and run away. Let's face it. I bullied my poor little sister. I think my parents would have stopped me but I was sneaky. I didn't tease her when they were around.

Of course a lot of "he said, she said" was going on. But to be fair to me, she wasn't easy to take. For one thing, Robbie was hyperactive. For another, she was into bugs. Girls aren't supposed to like bugs. When she was little I tried to scare her with bugs. I would throw a spider at her. She would laugh and throw it back at me. Then I realized she didn't like horror movies. That backfired on me too. One time I made her watch a scary movie. Robbie was so frightened that afterward she wouldn't stay alone. I had to babysit her for two years. What a nightmare—for me! Eventually, as I got older, I was too busy with my friends to spend any energy annoying her.

ROBIN

Harry was four years older than me. We fought a lot when we were little. Four years is a big difference when you are kids. He had to let his bratty little sister tag along. And I thought he was a bully. Always teasing me and doing mean things to me. For instance, when I was eight he tricked me into watching a scary movie on TV. I had to watch it because once I realized it was scary, I was too frightened to leave the room and be alone. That fear stayed with me for two years. Everything about the house scared me at night. Harry often got stuck babysitting me. We both remember that. However, as we got older we got along better. Sometimes I even liked him. And since I started high school when he started college, I think the separation of time and distance helped us to appreciate each other.

After Harry finished his B.A. at Cornell University, he went to MIT to study environmental engineering. He said he would find a new way to turn junk into energy and save the world. Okay, I admit it. I looked up to him. He could do anything he put his mind to.

MAGGIE (Mom)

I always wanted to make a difference for families and children. That's why I became a family law attorney and then a family court judge. I did my best to help all parties work out their disagreements for everyone's benefit. Especially the children. But as my disease progressed and my mobility decreased, I felt it best to resign. I still miss my work.

ROBIN

If everyone had Mom's attitude, this would be a great world. She had a positive outlook. Always made the best of every day and never complained. Always laughing. She read a lot, wrote articles on legal issues and took up painting. She and Dad socialized with their friends. She continued her volunteer work in our local school's mentoring program.

Dad had a swim spa pool installed in one of the spaces of our three-car garage. That way Mom could swim and exercise all year round. Still, seeing Mom struggling to do something physical was heartbreaking. But she never used her limitations as an excuse not to live a full and happy life. That was an important lesson for me.

MAGGIE (Mom)

I didn't feel sorry for myself. Well, maybe occasionally I allowed myself a little self-pity. However, my view is that we are not the same person all our lives. Our outlook, our attitude, even our personality traits can change with experience, education and age. Yes, I have a disability caused by MS. Yet I have been mentally and physically involved. Going places, socializing, volunteering, swimming, painting, writing.

And I was blessed with a beautiful, wonderful family. My husband, Bobby, is a loving, compassionate man. My children, Harry and Robbie, have been my support. Sometimes literally and always emotionally. Even as young adults, they shared their lives with me. Telling me what they were doing. What they were concerned about. Asking for my advice. And they are interesting and intelligent people. Harry with his passion for improving and saving the environment. Robbie with her devotion to the natural world, especially to insects.

ROBIN

I know I got my optimism from Mom. And my sense of purpose. And my commitment to social responsibility. By her example, she taught Harry and me social awareness and responsibility. She didn't just see injustice and unfairness. She tried to do something about it. Mom often said, "To whom much is given, much is expected." These weren't just words to her. My mom is my hero.

MAGGIE (Mom)

I've tried to instill in my children a sense of compassion and understanding for others. I've also tried to make them aware that their privileged upbringing isn't the norm for most people. Besides experiencing greater cultural and ethnic diversity when they visit my sister, Sue, in Brooklyn, we regularly volunteered. Delivering meals to needy families, mentoring homeless children, sharing food and our friendship at a homeless shelter. And Robbie discovered a charity called Swim for MS that raises money for research. She created her own swim challenges and was a top fundraiser twice.

BOBBY (Dad)

Robbie tended to spread herself a little thin with all her activities but she did have some balance in her life. It wasn't all insects and studies. She was a good kid with such a sweet and giving heart. The way she spent time with Maggie and helped her. Robbie tried to be her legs. Always cheerfully willing to do or get for her mother whatever was needed.

ROBIN

I read that insect colonies are considered by some scientists to be super-organisms because they function like cells in our bodies. The colony only survives and is healthy if all members do their part. And like the cells in our bodies, they must constantly be replaced with healthy members if the colony is to live. If I could find out what happens in a colony, maybe I could apply that information to what goes wrong in a person's body. And maybe there was an antidote for both. My hope was that someday I could learn enough from colony insects to help Mom.

MAGGIE (Mom)

I know how much Robbie wanted to help me. And everyone else with MS. Since it is an autoimmune disease, she believed studying insects might lead to a cure. Who knows? Maybe there is an answer there. Do insects get autoimmune diseases? Or do their colonies? I don't know but I was proud of her. Proud of both my children.

BOBBY (Dad)

I really thought that Robbie's interest in insects, especially social insects—ants, bees, wasps, termites—would just be a passing childhood phase. But since she was a little kid, she insisted she wanted to be an entomologist, a scientist who studies insects. It really surprised me that she maintained her passion for bugs. It was great she had a direction in life. I was also happy she outgrew her childish notion that she had some special power over insects.

ROBIN

Like all skills or powers, training was required. I didn't let other activities interfere with my "insect exercises." Colony insects were my first and most important focus. But to strengthen and expand my ability, I also practiced my mind control on other bugs.

During the summer evenings, I'd "think" mosquitoes away from me. I got good at it. Then I stopped mosquitoes from biting Mom and Dad. Dad even said it was strange that he no longer got the usual summer mosquito bites. But occasionally I would let one bite Harry. I know it was mean but it was funny to see him complain he was the only one who had gotten bitten. It became a game to me. I would stop moths from attacking my sweaters. I would stop flies from landing on food. My favorite was to make spiders leave the house. It made me feel good that these tiny lives—ones that were considered pests—didn't have to be killed just because they were doing their bug thing. And my family didn't need to use toxic pesticides. It was better and healthier for all of us.

HARRY (brother)
Robbie was so obsessed with insects that she wouldn't even kill one. When she was little she insisted we all use a suction thing to catch and release any crawling creatures—ants, spiders, beetles—that were inside the house. She said the only reason to kill a bug, or anything, was if it threatened someone. Like a mosquito that may be carrying a disease. I once saw her dispatch a mosquito she thought was going to bite Mom. But later, Mom and Dad and Robbie didn't seem to get mosquito bites. Most of the time, I didn't either. And except for Robbie's ant farm, there didn't seem to be any bugs in the house anymore. Anyway, as my interest in the environment grew I came to appreciate the interconnectivity of all living things. I guess Robbie and I had more in common than I thought.

ROBIN
I think that both Harry and I felt special. He was the only son. I was the only daughter. He was the firstborn and I, the only other child, was the baby of the family. Dad called

me "DD." Short for "Darling Daughter." He treated me with love and appreciation. Always willing to listen to my stories, my heartbreaks, my interests. I once read that a girl gets her self-esteem in relation to men from her father. My dad helped me value myself. And demand the respect that he showed me.

BOBBY (Dad)

When Robbie was very young I called her "Wild Girl." I was just joking about how hyperactive she was. But when she was diagnosed with ADHD, I felt terrible and stopped calling her that. Since then, she was my "Darling Daughter." And she called me her "Darling Dad."

Robbie had me wrapped around her little finger. There wasn't anything I wouldn't do for her. I guess most dads are like that with their daughters. Of course, my daughter *is* the best daughter in the world.

Brooklyn, New York

ROBIN

My parents were originally from New York City. After they got married they decided they wanted to raise a family in the country. Somewhere with a slower pace. They moved to Vermont. That's where Harry and I were born. But Mom and Dad were aware Vermont was lacking in people diversity. So they tried to expose us to the greater world. Every summer, Harry and I spent a month in Brooklyn with Mom's sister, Aunt Sue. We enjoyed big city life and the exposure to more ethnic diversity. But after Harry began an internship at an environmental engineering company, I went alone the summer before I started high school. I think that made me more open to meeting kids my age.

AUNT SUE (Maggie's sister)
I think Maggie and Bobby thought of me as "poor Sue" because I didn't have children. I certainly didn't think of myself that way. To begin with, I wasn't poor. My husband had died young—at 48—but not before he had made a lot of money as a hedge fund manager. Also, although I adored my niece and nephew, a month of their visits every summer and my holidays in Vermont were enough children for me. In fact, I counted myself lucky to have a close relationship with them but still be able to say goodbye when I wanted to.

Of course, as Robbie got older, we had more of an adult relationship. When she wasn't visiting me in Brooklyn, we often talked on the phone. I liked that she confided in me. And when the kids were visiting me, I did my best to expose them to all New York had to offer. Museums, theater, historical locations, different neighborhoods and different people. I think it's one reason they both chose to go to a big university. They liked all kinds of people and large numbers didn't intimidate them. But I can't take credit for Robbie and Brianna's friendship. They discovered each other all on their own.

BRIANNA (friend)
When I saw this lost-looking girl hanging around my building, I knew I had to help her. She was a fashion disaster. She was dressed like a lumberjack. Big plaid shirt, hiking boots, corduroy cargo pants. Oh please. Who wears corduroy cargo

pants? In the summer? And her hair was pulled together in something trying to be a knot but it was going in all directions at once. I brought her to my place where I began a complete overhaul. To her credit, she was a willing subject.

I don't think she had an appreciation for her physical gifts. Tall and thin. A pretty face. She had the striking combination of green eyes and dark red hair. I became obsessed with her transformation. I designed clothes for her. I styled her hair. She was my own model. When she went back to Vermont, her parents were shocked. They didn't recognize her. And her freshman year of high school was a big success. Instead of Annie Oakley, she had changed into Audrey Hepburn—my style icon—with black girl flair.

ROBIN

I made friends with Brianna, a girl close to my age who lived in my aunt's building. I thought she looked like a beautiful sienna Kate Middleton. She was cool. And worldly. She certainly improved my "Calamity Jane" sense of style. And she taught me the latest dances and what was the "in" music. We even played music together. All our favorite songs. Brianna on piano and me on a drum box. A step away from my ADHD drumming days.

But what I most liked about Brianna was how smart she was. She wanted to be a fashion designer. She planned on studying design and business because she said fashion was as much a business as an art. She was talented and clever. I knew she would be successful. We kept in touch during the year and she visited me every spring break. Brianna said her trips to Vermont exposed her to ethnic non-diversity.

BRIANNA (friend)

It's funny how you can find things in common with a person so different from you. Robbie was not judgmental of other people. I try to be that way. Not to judge a book by its cover. And she was open to trying different experiences and meeting different people. We challenged each other to find foods at least one of us had never eaten. Thai drunken noodles. Indian coconut rice. Mexican potato tacos. We rocked out to Missy Elliot and shared a love for Shakira. Robbie was also a big fan of Bo Diddley. She said that her brother and she discovered him when they were little kids. They liked his frenetic beat. I guess he became famous in the 1950s. So she introduced me to someone new.

I admit I was at first tentative about visiting Robbie in Vermont. I am such a city girl. But the place was awesome. Quiet and beautiful. Her house was spacious and un-crowded. Robbie had her own bedroom while I—in my parents' typical cramped New York apartment—was doomed to sharing a room with my sister.

Her parents were wonderful. I felt welcome. Her mom even painted my portrait. I just loved them. And her friends were great too. We'd sit in front of the fireplace eating pizza and talking girl talk. We'd go to their local hangout, Folino's, and eat more pizza. Robbie's friends were cool. They knew less about New York City life than she did. I was happy to share my experiences with them. But after a couple of weeks, I was ready to get back to the city. I missed the noise, the crowds, the dirty air.

MAGGIE (Mom)

Robbie and Harry went to private elementary and middle schools in Sherburne. Then they went to Champlain Valley Union High School, a public school. During those private school years, Robbie was introverted and withdrawn. Possibly it was her poor start in school. I think the other kids were put off by her hyperactivity. Even when her condition improved, she seemed to prefer the company of insects. She made an occasional friend here and there. But no one seemed to stick.

When Robbie was 13, she was surfing the internet and found Friendship Circle, an online group sponsored by a Jewish organization. We really liked what this organization stood for. It put teenage volunteers together with children who had distinctive needs. And that's how Robbie and Julie found each other. Julie's learning deficits required special education. Julie was lonely and Robbie understood the loneliness that results from being different. They spent hours together. Hiking, horseback riding, sailing on the lake. And Julie took an interest in Robbie's insects.

Robbie's social life changed in high school. Perhaps since those kids had no memory or preconceived idea of who she had been, she could make a fresh start. Whatever the reason, she had matured. Bright and intelligent, tall, willowy, big green eyes, thick auburn hair. But her new friends and popularity didn't affect her friendship or time spent with Julie.

Her friend Brianna was a positive influence. She helped Robin develop confidence in her appearance and in her ability to make friends. Brianna, being a city girl, did not find Robbie's insects appealing.

ROBIN

High school was a much better experience for me than elementary and middle school. I made new friends in high school. Both girls and boys. Our core group hung out together. Betsy, Allison, Sophia, Nolan and Simon. Nolan took me to my first prom in my sophomore year. I thought he was just doing the friend thing. But years later he told me he had a crush on me during our freshman and sophomore years. I was oblivious to whatever signals he was trying to give me. However, there was a guy in my class who I liked. Shawn. And he seemed unaware of my efforts to get his attention. "Hi Robin," was the only response I got. Turned out he was gay. I was clueless. Clearly I didn't understand girl and boy relationships. I played it safe by having a massive infatuation for every member of the boy band Backstreet Boys. Especially Nick Carter. It was pubescent "love" practice.

Anyway, I still considered Julie and Brianna my best friends. Julie had difficulty learning things. But there was nothing wrong with her understanding of friendship and fun. And even though I didn't say anything more to my parents about my ability to control insects, I did confide in Julie. She believed me. She trusted me. Just for fun I had her pick a direction for the bees to fly and I made them go that way. Julie was impressed. And Brianna was great. We talked all the time. I wished she lived closer. However, when we got together it was as if we had never been apart.

JULIE (friend)

I was different and being different often means being lonely. So when my parents signed me up for Friendship Circle and

I was paired with Robbie, it was the best day of my life. She became a true friend. She took away my loneliness. For the first time ever, I felt like I was fun to be with.

Robbie was special. She was smart. And beautiful. She could even control bugs like bees and ants. She showed me that you don't have to study bugs to know about them. You can learn a lot just by observing them. Thanks to Robbie, I developed an interest in insects.

When Robbie went to high school, she made new friends. They were like her. Smart and attractive. Not like me. Short and round and not very smart. Robbie said my five-feet, one-inch height was not that short. That I have the ideal woman's body for the nineteenth century. Ha ha. And that it was better to be "people smart" than book smart. Anyway, I was afraid Robbie would forget me. But she didn't. We talked to each almost every day. And if I left a message for her, she would always call me back. We still got together at least once a week. And she included me with her friends. Like when we all went to a rock concert in Burlington. She had nice friends and they were nice to me.

Even though I knew Robbie would go to college after high school, I was sure we would stay friends. And when she was away at college, she often invited me to visit her. Because of her, I felt more confident and likable. I even made a new friend at my school. But Robbie will always be my best friend.

WALDO (the dog)

"Robin was the most wonderful person in the whole world." Okay, dogs can't talk but I'd like to think that was what Waldo would have said about me. However, Waldo knew me better

than anyone else. He knew my faults. He saw me realistically. He would have told you how I made him wait on weekend mornings for his walk because I was too lazy to get up earlier. Or how his morning walks were usually short because I didn't allow enough time before I left for school.

He would complain that I only threw his ball a hundred times instead of the infinite number of throws he wanted. And I was messy. I'd leave my clothes on the floor of my room. But then I'd get upset because his nestling in them left my clothes covered with his fur. He would also tell you how I'd let him sleep on my bed but I wouldn't get up in the middle of the night to let him out when he—thankfully not often—had to pee. Then how I would be mad in the morning if he had peed by the door. But probably what he disliked most was all the time I spent with my insects or reading or fixing my hair instead of paying attention to him.

And Waldo could read my mind. He knew when I wanted to give him a bath so he wouldn't come when I called him. Actually, he almost never came when I called him. That was because I didn't really train him well. And because he was a Jack Russell terrier. A breed with a mind of its own. But when he was on my lap or he was snuggled next to me on my bed or I threw the ball for him or we were on our walks—everything was right with the world for both of us. I loved all animals but I loved Waldo the most.

4

TIME TO GROW UP

Camel's Hump State Park, Vermont

ROBIN
Julie and I liked to go hiking. We went many times to Mt. Philo State Park. It was close and the hikes were easy. We decided it was time for a more ambitious hike at Camel's Hump State Park. Dad took Harry and me there many times. It was less than an hour away. And with the second highest peak in Vermont, it was challenging.

JULIE (friend)
When Robin had a free school day in early March, she thought it was the perfect time for our hike to Camel's Hump. A weekday would be less crowded. And some snow would be better than the mud of April and May. I had school but my parents let me take the day off.

With Robin driving—off the three of us went. Robin and me and Waldo. We were outfitted with backpacks, warm jackets, hiking boots, snowshoes, a doggie coat and doggie booties. Yes, dogs were allowed. Although they had to be on a leash above the tree line. Just as we hoped, the park wasn't busy. But that didn't turn out well. What is the saying? "Be careful what you wish for."

ROBIN

When Julie and I and Waldo got to the park, we decided to go up on the Burrows Trail and come down on the Forest City Trail. Depending on how long we spent at the summit, it would take about six hours.

It was a clear, cool day. In the mid-40s. There were very few hikers in our part of the park or on the Burrows Trail. As we were going up the trail, we passed a middle-aged man coming down. He nodded and smiled a toothless grin as we hurried past him. He was one scary-looking guy. His clothes were filthy. He was unshaven with slicked back greasy hair. And he had a distinctively bad odor. I felt a shiver along my spine as he seemed to slither past us.

Julie felt the same way and—glancing back—whispered, "I'm glad we're going down the other trail."

When we reached the summit, it was beautiful. We took photos of the view and of each other holding Waldo. Proof we got there. On the way down the Forest City Trail—shortly after we reached the tree line—we were shocked to see the same guy sitting on a tree stump. He stood up and came over to us. My first thought was to run. But where? I looked around but there was no one else on the trail. Then he pulled out a gun. In that moment, I learned what it felt like to have your blood run cold.

"Hey, girlies," he said. "How about coming with me?"

It wasn't a request. And the way he said "girlies." I felt cheapened. Demeaned. I wasn't a young woman. I was just a "girlie." A nameless thing under his control because of the gun he held in his hand.

Julie was behind me. She was holding Waldo's leash. Without hesitation, Julie took off with Waldo. She ran into the woods that lined the trail just seven or eight feet away. I didn't know what to think. I felt relieved he didn't shoot her. That she and Waldo were safe. But I wished my cell phone was in her backpack instead of mine. And now I was alone with this man. My fear was intense.

"I didn't like the tubby one anyway," he sneered.

My voice quivered. "What do you want? I have $30. You can have it."

"Oh, I'll take it all right. But first we are gonna take a walk in the woods."

Then I saw Julie—my dear, brave friend—come out of the forest. Sneaking up behind him. Waldo wasn't with her. She had tied him up somewhere in the woods and he was barking madly. His racket was distracting. And hopefully it made the guy think she was still in the woods with Waldo.

I kept talking. Trying to keep his focus on me. "This is a bad idea," I said. "People know where we are. My friend has a cell phone and she is going to get help." But he was losing patience and started waving his gun at me. "She's not going to get a call out from here. And I'll be long gone before anyone shows up to help you. Go over there," he ordered, pointing the gun toward the woods on the opposite side of where Julie had run. By then Julie was close enough to take a swing at him with one of her snowshoes. He turned in time and deflected it before it hit him. Then he turned the gun on her and growled, "You little sow!"

I thought he was going to kill her. I ran forward and jumped on him. And Julie jumped on him too. We brought him down and tried to hold him on the ground. Our backpacks sliding from side to side made us off-balanced. He was able to push us off. But when we were wrestling with him, he dropped his gun. I grabbed it before he did.

He scrambled to his feet and ran into the woods. Toward where we heard Waldo barking. Julie and I ran after him. We didn't get very far before we saw him holding Waldo up by his harness. Poor Waldo. He was limp and helpless. The guy said, "Drop my gun and move back or I'm going to smash your dog against this tree. You'll have one dead dog."

I had the gun but I had never even held one before. My hands were shaking so much that I didn't think I would be able to shoot him and miss Waldo. I started talking. "Okay, okay. I'll give you your gun. Just don't hurt my dog," I blathered on. I was stalling for time while I summoned a whole army of ants. They aroused from their dormancy and left their nests. Thousands of them. And these were not the little ants that sometimes invade a house. They were big, black wood ants. I directed them to the warmth they needed. His body. Surging to him, they crawled up inside his pant legs.

At first, when he felt them, he shook one leg. Then the other leg. And then it became terribly apparent to him that he

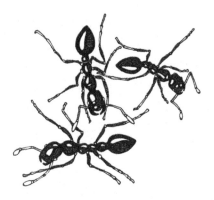

was being swarmed. He dropped Waldo and began swearing at the top of his lungs as he jumped around while swatting his legs. His slapping was useless. And with no other choice—he peeled off his pants. By then the ants were teeming over his body. Even his face, his ears, his hair. And they were biting. And spraying their formic acid into the bite wounds. Further increasing the pain. Yelling and cursing, he ran deep into the woods to escape the constant stream of ants rushing toward him.

Waldo, dragging his leash behind him, ran to us. Of course his leash snagged on a fallen branch. When we went to free him, Julie saw the guy's cast-off pants. She put on her gloves and then, with disgust, used just her forefinger and thumb to pick them up. She gleefully said, "He is not going to find them if he comes back here."

Constantly looking behind us, we went as fast as we could down the trail until we got to the Montclair Glen Lodge. Not really a lodge. Just a small cabin with a table and two bare wood bunk beds. It was built for stranded or tired hikers. There was a group of hikers in the little cabin. Four men and two women. Taking a break. They were shocked and furious when they heard our story. But they did have a laugh when they saw the guy's pants. A male hiker said, "He's gonna freeze his privates without those." Then one of the women searched the pant pockets and pulled out a car key. She was excited as she held it up for everyone to see. "He'll have a long walk home if he thinks he's going to get out of the park without his car key!"

We all went down the trail to the Trail's Head parking lot. The hikers told Julie and me to go to the Richmond police station and send the police back. They would search the lot for his car. They found a battered old car with dents and mismatched painted panels that fit his sleazy appearance. The car key fit.

The hikers waited for him. They knew who to look for. He would be the only man without pants. And when he showed up, the guy was freezing, pantless and not so tough without a gun. "What do you want with me? I didn't do nothin'," he protested. But it was one man against six adults. He didn't put up a fight. The hikers used their scarves to bind him. From the parking lot, they were able to make a cell phone call to the Richmond police. A squad car, with siren blaring, showed up in just 20 minutes.

JULIE (friend)
That was terrible. We could have been killed. And my parents were beyond upset. My mother said she shouldn't have let me take the day off from school. She would never again allow it. After what happened, that was okay with me.

I've always known that people could be cruel. I've felt it personally. But my parents taught me that every experience teaches you something. And the biggest lessons come from the worst happenings. What did I learn? First of all, just stay in school. Secondly, I learned it's usually safer to be where there are lots of other people.

Believe it or not, there were no phones, no visitor services and no rangers at Camel's Hump State Park. And very spotty cell service. After we got back to our car, we drove to the closest town, Richmond. We turned over the gun at the police station and made a report. While we were there, we learned the hikers did get the guy. The Richmond police were on their way to pick him up. We waited at the station to identify him. Just seeing the ghastly man again was unpleasant. But the police officers held him in check while he scowled at us.

We had to testify at his trial. And there he was. Not the dirty degenerate who had threatened us but a man who was all cleaned up. He was even wearing a full set of dentures. But the transformation didn't help him. He was convicted, cuffed and carted off to jail. No doubt a place he was well familiar with.

🍃 🍃 🍃

MAGGIE (Mom)
How naïve and trusting we were. Bobby and I made sure our children grew up protected. And we knew their world was a privileged one. One in which we thought no harm would come to them. Especially in a state park they had been to many times. The outside world shook us out of our fantasy. Our daughter, on the very cusp of adulthood, could have been taken from us.

Bobby was proud of how Robin defeated the thug. So was I. But I blamed myself for not preparing her for the realities of life. Evil does exist. Angry and hate-filled people do exist. People who need to control and belittle others for the dominance they crave. I saw it over and over in my own courtroom. Why didn't I make her more aware of the dangerous and sick people who live among us?

ROBIN

Mom and Dad blamed themselves for what happened at Camel's Hump. They said they should have better prepared me to be aware of dangerous people and unsafe situations. But I knew there were depraved people in the world. Except that it doesn't really hit home until you are personally facing serious injury or even death. I learned to be more mindful of everything and everyone around me. And I realized how fragile life—my life—is. I didn't want to waste my time on Earth. I wanted to be a force for good in this world.

BOBBY (Dad)

I shouldn't have let Robin and Julie go to Camel's Hump alone. It just never occurred to me that Robin, at 17, would be at risk going to a park she was familiar with. I had a lot of confidence in her maturity and ability to take care of herself. And despite the challenging circumstances, she proved me right. She, with Julie's help, managed to overcome a ruthless man.

But after we heard the story I was still unclear as to why the guy took his pants off. In court, he said he was attacked by thousands of ants. That was odd. Ants basically hibernate during cold weather. It's called diapause. And even if some ants were active, that doesn't explain the numbers he described. And what was it that attracted the ants him? It was strange. Or was it?

🍃   🍃   🍃

ROBIN

After that extremely unpleasant and scary experience, I was happy to concentrate on school. I kept busy. I worked at getting good grades because I wanted to get into Cornell University, Harry's school. I continued to take the AP—Advanced Placement—courses. My favorite subjects were science, biology, chemistry and math. I was on the girls' track team. I played the snare drums in the marching band. Both were good outlets for my residual hyperactivity. And just like Harry I also rowed crew on the school's co-ed team. We rowed on Lake Champlain in the fall before winter hit with snow and temperatures below freezing.

I didn't date much. For one thing until my junior year, I towered over most of the boys in my class. I thought Nolan would ask me again to our junior prom. And he did. But too late. Another boy, Roger, asked me first and I accepted. Roger was a good guy and I had a nice time. Still I regretted not waiting a little longer. And I was sorry I hadn't just asked Nolan. I would have had more fun with him. Anyway, Nolan and I didn't make the same mistake for senior prom. We asked each other at the same time and laughed at how we messed up the year before. Although we had a blast at our senior prom, it was a little bittersweet. We all knew we were going to different colleges in the fall. We'd remain friends but no more hanging out at Folino's Pizza or cheering together at the football and basketball games. Or cruising up and down the main street of our village. We were a good bunch of kids. And, as I said, Sherburne was a great place to grow up. A golden place. Throw in good parents and I could almost forget there were terrible people in the world.

NOLAN (friend)

I did have a crush on Robbie during our freshman year but I was an insecure nerd. I was more comfortable with math than with girls. I found socializing in a group easier. And even though Robbie was taller than me until my senior year, that wasn't what bothered me. What bothered me was that she won the school's science fair during our freshman year. I was flabbergasted and intimidated. Her experiment was about how plants promote pesticide breakdown. Mine had to do with how different objects can be measured with accuracy. Robbie's was more advanced and took a week to do. Mine was a beginner level and took only a day. The competition was on. The next year I put in much more effort. I took first place with an algorithm for solving a Rubik's Cube. Robbie got second place with an ecological footprint analysis. Our junior year I won again with a fractals study and Robbie took third place with her invasive species project. Finally, in our senior year, Robbie's colony bee collapse experiment won first place and I got second place with my science of catapult statistics study.

Clearly, we were two competitive people. But it was fun to challenge each other. Every year we tried to hide what our projects were. And we'd get our friends to spy for each of us. Our rivalry was fun. My crush on Robbie evolved into a great friendship. We enjoyed each other's company and had a lot of laughs.

Ithaca, New York

ROBIN

I was accepted to Cornell University. Sophia and Simon wanted small schools close to home. Sophie went to Middlebury College and Simon went to Bennington College. Allison took a break year to travel before starting college. Betsy went to the University of Vermont. Nolan went to the University of Pennsylvania. And Brianna—who was a year older than me—was already at the Fashion Institute of Technology in New York.

I had conflicting feelings. I was happy to be going away to school. I was sad to be leaving Mom and Dad and Waldo. But when you are young and ready to spread your wings, it is a thrilling time in your life. And Dad promised to take excellent care of Waldo. That meant throwing the ball for him and letting him sleep on their bed. Anyway, I'd be home for holidays and summer vacations. And I wasn't so far away that I couldn't come home for occasional weekends.

As a freshman, I had to choose my dorm. I applied to Ecology House and was accepted. There were 96 coeds. And the one thing we all had in common was a passion for preserving and protecting the environment. I shared a double room with a private bathroom. My roommate was Blair, a girl from Carmel, California. We got along great. She became my closest friend at school. I majored in entomology and minored in biology. Blair majored in Environmental and Sustainability Science because her goal was to become an environmental lawyer.

I joined the Snodgrass and Wigglesworth Undergraduate Entomology Club. SnodWiggs for short. The club had fun activities like bake sales, guest speakers, camping trips and infamous barbecues. Even though Blair didn't share my passion for insects, I talked her into joining for the club's activities. And when Julie or Brianna visited me, I took them to the club events.

I loved college. It was everything I wanted it to be. I was on my own, the bills were being paid and all I had to do was learn. I like to learn. What could be better?

BLAIR (friend and roommate)
Robbie and I became friends immediately. We were attuned to many of the same interests. Obviously, the environment was one of them. The only complaint I had about Robbie was that she tended to be disorganized. I was a neat freak. But we worked it out. She kept her mess on her side of the room and on her bathroom vanity cart. And I bought a hand vacuum to clean up hair from the bathroom floor. Because she was a good roommate and a considerate person, she used it.

Since I wanted to be a good roommate too, I joined Robbie's club, SnodWiggs. She reciprocated by joining my club choice, Human Ecology's Prelaw Undergraduate Society. But I have to admit, it was about as enjoyable as its name suggested. Not much. The SnodWiggs activities were fun and I enjoyed going to them.

ROBIN

As close as Blair and I became, I never told her about my ability to control bugs. To begin with, I didn't want her to think she had a crazy roommate. And she was so meticulous. I didn't want her to worry that I would invite many-legged creatures into our room.

BLAIR (friend and roommate)

Robbie had a good sense of humor. She said she got it from her father. She loved practical jokes. Like the time we were having beers with some guys in a campus bar. She bet one of the guys that he couldn't balance a glass of beer on the back of each hand as his hands rested on the table. When the guy managed to balance them, we just walked out. I'll never forget the look on his face as we were leaving. We heard later that he figured out how to drink both glasses down. He wasn't going to waste two beers.

When we weren't overwhelmed with studies, exams and papers, we occasionally went to a campus party. And sometimes we went on dates. But neither of us drank much so we didn't fit into the party crowd. I think we were good company. Intelligent and fun and funny. But we weren't interested in relationships at that time. We were focused on our studies and our goals. We probably didn't give the "I'm open to connecting" vibe. And with lots of friends in Ecology House and SnodWiggs to hang with, we weren't starving for camaraderie.

Then in our junior year we moved off campus to an apartment in the Collegetown area. Since it was a two-bedroom apartment, friends of ours from SnodWiggs—Aaron and Cory—joined us. They were good guys. And their share of rent helped when I took my junior year spring semester abroad in Italy. Robbie decided she wasn't ready to be that far away from family—especially her mom—for that long. Instead she took a winter insect ecology and behavior intersession course at La Selva Biological Station in Costa Rica. They did insect surveys, learned collecting, observational and experimental methods. She was in heaven just anticipating it.

Costa Rica

ROBIN

The first week at the La Selva Biological Station was great. There were so many insects in the jungle. I was in my element. Everyone was amazed that I didn't have to douse myself in insect repellent. I told them that biting bugs didn't like me. And if they were around me they wouldn't need repellents. But only a couple of kids were brave enough to forgo spraying themselves. Of course, we few were fine because I kept the biting bugs away.

The second week at La Selva was a disaster for me. While I was home for Christmas vacation, it was obvious that something was wrong with Waldo. The vet said that Waldo, then 16 years old, was experiencing kidney failure and would probably live only three or four more months. I was devastated. But I knew my family would take good care of him while I was away. And I was counting on him to still be alive when I got back from Costa Rica. Then Harry called to tell me Waldo had taken a turn for the worse. He was at the animal hospital. Slowly and painfully dying. Harry wanted to know if they should try to keep him alive until I could get home in ten days.

I desperately wanted to be there. To hold and comfort Waldo when he took his last breath. But my dying dog was not considered an emergency and the group travel arrangements didn't allow me to fly home alone. I knew Waldo was suffering. I couldn't be that selfish. I told Harry to go ahead and have Waldo euthanized. I tried to Skype so I could see my little love's face one last time. And maybe he would recognize my image. But the connection failed. Harry held Waldo when it was done. My heart was broken. I cried for three days. I could hardly see anything—even insects—through my flood of tears. Thankfully, my fellow students were understanding and supportive.

🍃 🍃 🍃

BLAIR (friend and roommate)

In our Collegetown apartment, Cory and Aaron shared a bedroom and bathroom. Robin and I had the other suite. Robbie and I were firm believers that if you room with men, you keep it platonic. Which is one of the reasons why the boys were good roommates. We weren't attracted to them. And they both had serious girlfriends. Aaron was from New York City. A great guy. An intelligent guy. Cory was from Baltimore. He was also smart and a real sweetheart.

Just after I left for my spring semester abroad, Aaron brought over a friend. His name was David. Robbie and David were immediately attracted to each other. And while I was in Italy, they started dating and developed a relationship. I think he was the first serious boyfriend Robbie had ever had. But by the time I got back in May, it was over. I could see she was hurt and disappointed but she didn't want to talk about it. That's usually a sign of self-blame and shame. We had roomed together for three years. We were close friends. I insisted she tell me what had happened.

Robbie said she had really fallen for David. He was studying electrical engineering. Her father's field. He was good-looking. He was fun. He seemed nice. But "seemed" is the operative word here. Anyway, she began to imagine a future together. Then—thank goodness—David revealed his "real" self. He made fun of her interest in insects and her future career in entomology. He said there was no money to be made in her field. At first it was good-natured but then he got nastier. Like telling her not to tell his friends she wanted to be an entomologist because it wasn't feminine. As if he was embarrassed by her and her future profession. That was cruel. After all, entomology was an important part of Robbie's identity.

And he always pressured Robbie to change her plans to what he wanted to do. But it was hard for her to give up on the fantasy. Then he did the unforgivable. He purposely stomped on some beetles right in front of her. "For fun," he said. He knew it went against everything she believed in. He laughed at how it upset her. Robbie said she finally realized how little he respected her—much less cared about her. She broke it off.

ROBIN

I should have told Blair right away about how hurt and humiliated I was. After all, Blair was my close friend. But the whole experience with David made me feel like a loser. It made me doubt myself. Why did it take me so long to remember my father's lesson about the importance of respect?

Blair was understanding and supportive. She told me about her horrible relationship experience. And about her other girlfriends' dreadful boyfriends. At first I thought, "Are girls just idiots when it comes to boys?" But the more we talked, the more we both realized these are the lessons of life most people go through. If a woman recognizes and ends an emotionally or physically abusive relationship in time—she will be stronger and smarter.

BLAIR (friend and roommate)

David wouldn't accept it was over. He basically stalked Robbie. Showing up outside her classes. Taking the same yoga class. Even joining SnodWiggs. He couldn't or wouldn't accept she didn't want to be with him anymore. He was a future woman abuser.

AARON (roommate)

Psychological abuse is as harmful as physical abuse. And since it often leads to the latter, I think Blair was wrong about David being a "future" woman abuser. He had already earned that appalling title.

CORY (roommate)

David was stalking Robbie. She wanted to handle it herself.

But Aaron felt responsible for introducing them. And we both felt protective of Robbie and Blair. They weren't just our roommates. They were our friends. So Aaron and I had a little talk with David and told him things would get real unpleasant real fast if he didn't leave Robbie alone. I don't know if we actually would have done anything to him. But one thing I have learned is that abusive people are genuine cowards. Anyway, the important thing is he believed us and he stayed away from her. She was well rid of him. We all were.

ROBIN

After Cornell, I wanted to go to graduate school in the West. Specifically, I was interested in the University of California, Davis. The school had started as an agricultural college in the early twentieth century and had grown to a full-blown university with integrated programs in my sciences—entomology, immunology and biophysics. With my strong undergraduate background in these areas, I felt comfortable going straight for a doctorate.

Blair's description of California—especially the weather, the weather and the weather—was an added motivation. And I felt truly ready for somewhere unlike the East Coast. Also, Blair was going to law school at the University of California, Berkeley. Davis and Berkeley weren't far from each other.

I discussed it with Mom and Dad. They were encouraging. And while Mom wasn't doing better, at least she wasn't doing worse. I applied and was ecstatic when I got an acceptance letter.

MAGGIE (Mom)

Of course, we didn't really want Robbie to go far away for graduate school. When she was at Cornell, she was close enough to easily come home for holidays and sometimes on weekends. We hoped she would pick an eastern school. But UC Davis was a good school and a good fit for her. That's what mattered.

We would never make her feel she couldn't do something she wanted to do because of us. It was her life. We raised her to be an independent and strong person. She had to follow her passion. Wherever that led her. We felt Robbie had a purpose. We believed she would achieve her goals and do something special in her life.

BOBBY (Dad)

We certainly wanted her to stay closer. We just hoped she wouldn't fall in love with someone on the West Coast or some-day get a job there. We wanted her to eventually return east.

MAGGIE (Mom)

Yes. We just hoped she wouldn't stay out there.

5
—

STEPS AND MISSTEPS

Davis, California

Davis is located 15 miles from Sacramento, the capital of California, and 74 miles from San Francisco. It is a town of 66,000. When in session, the university adds an additional 35,000 students—just over one-half the size of the town. A true college town.

JAMIE (Jinsong's English name)

I was excited when my plane landed in San Francisco. I was really in the United States. A new adventure. A new stage of my life. I planned to spend four days touring the city before catching a bus to Davis. And I made sure to see a lot of the usual tourist sights.

San Francisco was a beautiful city. Diverse and busy. The view of the bay was spectacular. And best of all was fresh, clean air. I walked a lot. Even going up the famous steep hills. I went to Chinatown. It didn't remind me of home but I did have a good dim sum there at a little restaurant called Hang Ah. I went to the Asian Art Museum and the Museum of Modern Art, to Fisherman's Wharf, walked the Golden Gate Bridge, rode a cable car and walked to North Beach. But after three days, I decided it was time to go to Davis. I was eager to get started on my education. And on my future. In an over two-hour bus ride, I noted the smaller and small cities. Berkeley, Richmond, Vallejo, Fairfield, Vacaville and finally Davis. When entering Davis, a posted sign listed the population and the elevation above sea level—52 feet. I thought that was funny since Chinese cities don't do that.

Davis was pleasant. It was smaller than Guilin. But I had a good idea of what to expect. I had done a lot of online research including looking at hundreds of photos. It was a new experience to be in a city that was considered a "college town." Very different from attending Tsinghua University and living in gigantic Beijing.

The first thing I wanted to do was to find my residence. The second thing was to get a bicycle—the most popular mode of student transportation. I had applied for a studio apartment at a complex for graduate students called the Atriums. I had never lived alone. I decided I wanted to give it a try. I wasn't worried about being lonely because I knew I would meet students in my classes. Also, I had looked up school clubs and organizations. I was amazed to find that there were 800. Chinese universities do not encourage student associations. Tsinghua had about 200 organizations. And since those were supervised by the school's Communist Youth League Committee, many students avoided joining them. I knew there were many Chinese students at Davis. Even two Chinese student clubs. But I wanted to meet new people who were from unfamiliar places, backgrounds and cultures.

When I got to my studio apartment, I was pleasantly surprised. I hadn't realized 500 square feet would feel so big. Besides having a kitchen and a bathroom, it also had a patio. I expected one big room but a wall separated the bedroom from the main living area. That meant I could have friends over without my bed having to double as a couch. I was lucky to get the last studio available.

LING (Mother)

I received a text from Jinsong. He wanted to let me know he was in Davis. His text was full of happy information. His apartment was much nicer than he expected. He was getting himself moved in. Setting up his computer, buying groceries and purchasing a bicycle. It was green. His favorite color. He said bicycle paths were everywhere on the campus and in the town. One bike trail even circled most of the city.

He had no trouble talking to people in conversational English. Everyone was friendly and helpful. Every minute of these new experiences made him feel happy. I was relieved and thankful to learn his news.

JAMIE

On my first bike ride I explored downtown Davis—essentially part of the campus—and the restaurants located there. I found an Italian restaurant, Paesanos. Both the pizza and the pasta were good. I knew I would eat there often. I was familiar with Italian food from many pasta dinners with the Kindles. Later I tried a couple of the Chinese restaurants. But they served the Americanized version of Chinese food. Not what I was used to.

Though I had already received approval from the doctoral committee to pursue an interdisciplinary degree in botany and biology, I met with my faculty advisor to decide on my first semester courses. Then I located the buildings where my classes would be held.

SYLVIA (Jamie's faculty advisor)

Jamie Chen was worried the English instruction might be difficult for him. I found his English to be satisfactory. I didn't think he would have any problem in his classes. But I recommended he start with the usual three courses. I wanted to make sure he was well accustomed to the course-work before he increased his class load. We decided he would start with one elective and two core courses. Approaches in Quantitative Analysis in Life Sciences, Microbial Metabolism and Critical Thinking for Life Sciences. Quantitative Analysis is a math course. A subject he said he always enjoyed and excelled at.

ROBIN

After many tears and even buying my return ticket home for Thanksgiving, I left for Davis, California, right after Labor Day. First I visited Blair. She was already situated at University of California, Berkeley. She showed me the Berkeley campus and then we explored San Francisco.

BLAIR (friend)

I grew up in Carmel. I had been to San Francisco many times during my childhood. I knew exactly what I wanted Robin to see and do. All my favorite kid and teenage experiences.

We shopped in North Beach and Union Square, took the cruise to Alcatraz, had afternoon tea at the Palace Hotel, went to the top of Coit Tower on Telegraph Hill to take in the amazing view, took a cable car to the Ferry Building and had Irish coffee at the Buena Vista Café. We saw a concert at The Fillmore. The place had been around since the 1970s. We also had a good dim sum in Chinatown. In a little restaurant tucked away in an alley. Hang Ah Tea Room. It had been there forever.

ROBIN

We had a great time. I was happy that my school was close to San Francisco. I could take trips to the city. And to the Wine Country and the Gold Country. I was looking forward to discovering more of California and the beautiful West Coast. But after five days, it was time for me to go. Blair's friend, Trevor, drove us to Davis. It was a pleasant two-hour drive through rolling hills and past small cities. Some had quaint "old town" sections.

When we got to Davis, we were all impressed with the charming college town. The campus was pretty. And large. But having attended Cornell, I was used to a big school. It seemed as if everyone was on a bike. Even the traffic lights had a special signal for bicycles. Then we drove to my residence. A private apartment building called Viridian. It wasn't my first choice. I had decided that it was time for me to live alone. I tried to get a studio apartment at the on-campus Atriums. But just an hour before I called someone got the last available one. The only other option at the Atriums was a two-bedroom. That was more cost and space than I wanted or needed. The Viridian offered one and two-bedroom apartments. I got a one-bedroom.

BLAIR (friend)

The Viridian lived up to its pretty name. It had a fitness center with a yoga room, a sand volleyball court, outdoor kitchens, grilling areas and fireplaces, study lounges and two pools. One was a lap pool. I hoped she would have time to make use of all the amenities.

Robbie would have preferred to have been on the campus but Viridian was only about a half mile away. And it was close to the town bike loop. At almost 800 square feet, her apartment was roomy and comfortable. It even had a balcony where she could keep a bicycle. I was a little jealous. My place at Berkeley was a shoebox by comparison. Anyway, Trevor and I were impressed with the place.

ROBIN

We all had dinner together at Paesanos, an Italian restaurant in the campus town. It was good. I put the restaurant's information in my phone notes. I had become a vegetarian while I was at Cornell. I ate lots of pasta, vegetables and salads. I did eat fish. And sometimes I cheated when I had a craving for bacon. So it would be more accurate to say I was a "flexitarian."

After Blair and Trevor left to go back to Berkeley, I began to settle in. I called my parents. Something I did most every day. I set up my computer, put away some clothes and went out for groceries. I had arrived! I bought a bike the next day. I picked out a green one. I thought that was fitting since Davis is a green campus. Besides, it matched my green eyes. Then I met with my graduate faculty advisor.

SYLVIA (Robin's faculty advisor)

It was Robin's intention to finish the doctoral coursework as fast as possible. We set the direction for the next three years. She already had approval from the doctoral committee to pursue an interdisciplinary Ph.D. in entomology and biology. That way she could do research relating her entomology curriculum to human health and disease. As I usually do, I recommended she take three courses the first semester. Two core classes and one elective. Get her feet on the ground before she expanded her class load.

I thought Robin was extremely well-prepared for the Insect Behavior course. But she felt the class would offer the latest academic research. She also registered for Insect Molecular Biology and Approaches in Quantitative Analysis in Life Sciences.

ROBIN

I had a week before classes started on September 21. I explored the campus, the library, the town. I hung out at my building. Swimming, using the yoga room and the fitness center. I joined a daily volleyball game. I was not a great volleyball player but my height was an asset at the net.

One thing about college and being young is that it's easy to make friends. People are open and friendly. While playing volleyball I met two girls I liked. Anne and Francis.

ANNIE (new friend)

I was from Glen Ellen, California, and my roommate Francis was from Tulsa, Oklahoma. ASUCD Community Housing had connected us and we were sharing a two-bedroom apartment. I was getting my doctorate in viticulture. Having grown up in the heart of the Wine Country, Napa Valley, wine production was my passion. Francis was working on her doctorate in computer science. Eventually, she wanted to work in Silicon Valley.

She hoped she could get a job at Google because she knew someone who knew someone who worked there.

Big surprise. Everyone called us Annie and Frannie. And sometimes we were referred to as just Annie/Frannie. We joked that if we knew that was going to happen we wouldn't have roomed together.

ROBIN

Okay, I admit I'm the one who started the Annie/Frannie thing. It's my sophomoric sense of humor. However, I was a little hypocritical because I introduced myself to everyone as Robin. It felt more grown-up than Robbie. Anyway, a lot of graduate students lived at Viridian and there was an easy camaraderie.

🍃 🍃 🍃

JAMIE

I was sitting on my patio enjoying the sunshine and eating a bun filled with blueberries. It reminded me of a heavier and sweeter version of a Chinese fruit-filled bun. I put the bun down on my outdoor table and went in to get a pot of tea. When I returned, the bun was gone. I was perplexed. What happened to it? Then I heard the cawing of a crow. I looked up and saw the bird sitting in the loquat tree just outside my patio wall. My bun was in its beak. I was joking

when I yelled, "Give it back." But then I heard the tree say, "Give it back!" And it wasn't joking. I was shocked when the crow flew down and dropped the roll at my feet. I asked the tree how it did that. It told me that trees and birds have a mutual relationship. If the crow wanted to know which was the sweetest fruit, it had to obey the tree and return my stolen roll.

I certainly didn't want to eat the roll anymore. But I was enjoying my tea when I heard a person say, "Hello." It was a guy who was on his patio just across from mine. We started talking. He was interested in my being from China. I was interested in his being from Los Angeles. His name was Jake. We decided to get a coffee at the University Mall's corner Starbucks.

JAKE (new friend)

I had just arrived from Los Angeles after driving for six hours without a break. I was getting a Ph.D. in computer science. I told Jamie that I could hack into most anything. I wanted to go into cybersecurity. Maybe even start my own company. I didn't really think I needed a Ph.D. but I liked school and I wanted the credibility that the title of "doctor" bestows.

JAMIE

Who couldn't use good cybersecurity? There had to be great need in that field. I wondered if I would find as much opportunity in my field.

JAKE (new friend)

I told Jamie Los Angeles was massive. He said I should see Beijing if I wanted to see massive. We exchanged stories about our countries, our families, our past girlfriends. Regarding the latter, I seemed to have had many more relationships than he did. He only mentioned his high school sweetheart, Lijuan. We talked for a couple of hours before I decided I had to "crash." A new term for Jamie. From there our friendship easily developed.

JAMIE

After my first week at UC Davis, I was surprised to feel home-sick. Maybe it was because I had too much time on my hands since classes hadn't started. I decided to visit the Chinese Student Union and the Chinese Union. Both clubs were pleasant. The students there were nice. And it was good to speak Mandarin again. But I felt most of them would rely on their fellow Chinese for a social life. I didn't want to do that.

As I biked around the campus, I saw that most students stuck with their own ethnic group or racial group. I understood the need for the comfort and sense of identity that comes with familiarity. But I wanted to learn about everyone.

The International House was on the list of organizations. I decided to check it out. It was in a renovated two-story historic house. I liked the place right away. I found people who were open to others with different backgrounds. The first people who greeted me were a couple from Karachi, Pakistan. Bilial and Amira Jalbani. They were warm and funny. Especially Amira. She said Bilial wanted to return to Pakistan after they completed their doctorates but no way was she going back.

"I like it here," Amira told me. "I let Bilial tell me what to cook. But otherwise no man is going to give me orders like most men in Pakistan who dominate the women." Bilial laughed. "She wants to stay here because she is the boss here," he said. "We'll see who gets the better job when we graduate and who wears the pants in the family then." They both laughed. Their marriage was obviously based on respect and an easygoing humor. They introduced me to some other people there. One was a British woman, Alicia. We had an enjoyable conversation and exchanged cell phone numbers.

AMIRA (new friend)

Bilial and I were close to finishing our doctorates. We just had our dissertations approved in our respective fields. Neuroscience for me and applied mathematics for him. Writing them would be our last steps.

It could be said that our marriage was arranged by our families but it was more of an introduction. We had the final say. Happily, we liked each other right away. Bilial was a modern man. He was raised in a progressive family. He thought women should be equal to men. I couldn't be with any man who didn't think that way. Having my own career and identity was always important to me.

Maybe it was because our marriage worked out well that I believed it was good to have an interested person evaluate prospective partners. And I admit I did like to play matchmaker. So when I met Jamie, I wanted to help him find someone special. I didn't think it would be difficult. He was smart and pleasant and good-looking. At the International House I introduced him to Alicia. A very nice young woman. But I would keep looking for someone for him if that didn't work out.

JAMIE

The last weekend before classes started Jake wanted to drive to the Gold Country. It was northeast of Davis. He invited his friend, Brian, and me. We left early since we wanted to see a couple of towns. Sutter Creek, Placerville. I enjoyed the drive. The landscape was golden rolling hills dotted with green trees and broken up with little gullies and valleys filled with oak woodlands. The trees spoke to me about how much they liked the climate of California. I agreed.

Sutter Creek was where gold in California was first discovered. Though the historic one and two-story wood buildings were mostly filled with tourist shops, it met my expectation of an old Western town. The main street was on a gently sloping hill. Sometimes the sidewalks had steps up and down. Most of the stores had wooden overhangs in front of the windows and doors. Good for avoiding the sun. I liked the place. Different from small towns in China.

🍃 🍃 🍃

ROBIN

Annie had a car. She suggested that we do something fun on our last weekend before we started the grind of classes and studying. Frannie and I wanted to see the Gold Country. Just over an hour drive. So that Saturday we drove to Sutter Creek. What a lovely area. I could just imagine the miners sifting for gold in all the creeks that laced the gullies and the craggy canyons. The town was delightful. The namesake creek ran just behind the downtown buildings.

A lot of the stores were touristy but still charming. Frannie wanted to find a frog figurine to add to her collection while Annie hunted for something that was wine related. In one shop I was unexpectedly drawn to a dragonfly pendant. I don't know why but I had to buy it.

After we explored the five or six blocks of the main street, we decided to eat at Buffalo Chips. The name itself made it worth eating there. It was a yellow corner building that had once been a house. Now its spaces were divided into different eating rooms. As we were entering the restaurant, Frannie waved to someone across the street. I turned to look but all I glimpsed were three guys walking away. One was tall with collar-length black hair. Anyway, the food was good. Annie/Frannie had burgers. I had a veggie sandwich.

JAMIE

Brian and I were hungry. But Jake wanted to go to a Placerville restaurant. A place he found on Yelp called the Heyday Café. We were walking back to the car when Jake waved to a girl he knew from his computer classes. I saw three girls together. One was tall. They were going into a restaurant that looked appealing. I wished we were eating there. Placerville was 40 minutes away. But since he who drives gets to make the decisions—we left for the Heyday Café. I was starving by the time we got there. It was a small storefront restaurant. Maybe six low tables on one side of the room and the same number of high tables on the opposite side. I ordered a pizza and ate it all. Jake and Brian had panini sandwiches. I was so hungry that anything would have tasted good. But the pizza was delicious.

Next we explored the town's main street. Placerville's downtown was different from Sutter Creek. Bigger and busier. About eight or nine blocks. More original two-story brick buildings. The street was flat so the sidewalks didn't need steps to accommodate a slope. It was an interesting town.

ROBIN

I was ready for classes to start. Ready to get going. Insect Behavior and Insect Molecular Biology were stimulating. Both covered the most current science. We entomology students bonded over our common interest. And we knew we would see each other in various classes over the next two to three years.

A guy in the Molecular Biology class was clearly interested in me. I would have reciprocated his attention but he looked like my brother Harry. And even though I think Harry is nice looking, it felt creepy for a possible romantic interest to resemble him. Also, his name was David. Two strikes against him.

Quantitative Analysis was an interdisciplinary class. Basically a math class. I'm good at math. But, of course, I enjoyed my entomology classes more. The QA class was in a lecture hall with stadium seating. There were probably over 100 students. Maybe slightly more girls than boys.

JAMIE

I found the Microbial Metabolism course challenging and my other courses informative. Thankfully, I didn't find the language difference to be a problem. I liked my Quantitative Analysis course. It was an easy class for me. I always sat in the front row, left side. It is funny how students tend to stick with the same seat in a class. As I looked down my row, I saw the top of a woman's head. Just her hair. It was a reddish-brown color. Auburn. Not a common natural hair color. I remember wondering if I had seen her before. I wanted to see her face but I couldn't find her in the rush of students leaving when class was over. I forgot about looking for her again.

ROBIN

As I did in all my classes, I looked around the QA class to see who else was there. Since I was sitting in the front all the way to the right, I couldn't see everyone behind me or even entirely down my row. I didn't or couldn't see any GOI. My acronym for "Guys Of Interest." When the class was over and everyone filed out, I noticed a tall man with black straight hair that was long enough to cover his shirt collar. But I could only see the back of his head. I felt a sense of familiarity. Had I met him before? It was an odd feeling.

JAMIE

Two weeks later I was chaining my bicycle up to the rack outside the building for the Quantitative Analysis class when the girl with auburn hair rode up on a green bicycle. As she chained her bike, we looked at each other. I was startled by her bright green eyes. The color of a pothos plant leaf. I had never seen that eye color before. And she was pretty. In fact, I thought she was beautiful. And tall. Maybe just two or three inches shorter than me. Her hair was long. But not too long as to have that messy, stringy look. I was staring at her when she said hello. I felt unnerved. And like a confused idiot I just nodded and quickly went inside. After that awkward meeting I looked for her in class. She was always sitting on the opposite end of my row. I realized she was the girl with auburn hair I noticed the first day of class. I wanted to talk to her but I felt embarrassed at how clumsily I had acted. She must have thought I was unfriendly or rude. I thought my shyness with girls—with this girl—was back.

ROBIN

When I was locking my bike before a class, a guy with longish black hair was also securing his bike. I felt an immediate sense of recognition. Of familiarity. I was sure I had seen him somewhere. I said hello. But he just stared at me and then rushed into the building. He was Asian. Maybe he was uncomfortable with American girls. Or maybe he didn't speak English well. Or maybe he wasn't into girls. Whatever the reason, I was sorry we didn't talk. He was amazing looking. And several inches taller than me. Definitely over six feet. Afterward I would look for him in class. He was always sitting at the other end of my row. I never saw him look my way. Why was it so hard to meet a guy I might be interested in?

JAMIE

The students in my classes were friendly. I exchanged cell numbers with some of them. As the quarter progressed I was more confident about my ability to handle my courses and exams. I felt comfortable about taking some time for a social life. Usually on weekends, Jake and I would go out for beers or coffees or burgers. Sometimes Brian joined us. And Alicia and I went on dates. She was nice but I didn't feel a special attraction. Still, she was good company and I was comfortable with her. I began to wonder if I could only be relaxed with a girl who was just a friend.

AMIRA (friend)

When Bilial and I next saw Jamie at the International House, I wanted to know how his relationship with Alicia was going. He told us they were dating but he didn't think they would be more than friends. I said I would keep looking for the right young woman for him. I think that embarrassed him because he said he was too busy with his studies to be serious about anyone. But his evasion didn't deter me from my mission.

FRANNIE (friend)

Annie and I were hanging out at the volleyball court waiting for a game to form. I called Robin to see if she wanted to play. She said she had stubbed her big toe. It hurt too much to play but she would come down to cheer for us. Once there, she joined the small group of people who were watching. Robin's a friendly, outgoing person. She started talking to some of the other onlookers. Especially a couple from Pakistan who lived in our building. I wasn't surprised to see her having a conversation with them. She loved meeting people from all over the country and the world. She considered me exotic because I was from Tulsa, Oklahoma. After the game, the three of us—Robin, Annie and I—went for coffee. Robin said the couple she met was super nice and interesting. She exchanged cell numbers with the woman.

ROBIN

I met this great couple from Pakistan. They also lived at the Viridian. I asked if they were Muslim and she, Amira, said they were. I asked why she wasn't wearing a hijab. She told me that she only wore one when she went to the mosque. She explained, "I love God and I love my religion. A scarf on my head doesn't make me more religious." I was surprised. It seemed to me that all the young Muslim women at Cornell and UC Davis wore hijabs.

Amira said, "It's more than just being religious. It's an identity thing. And sometimes maybe peer pressure or parental pressure. And besides, they might be advertising what good Muslim girls they are. Maybe even husband hunting. I've already got a husband." Amira and her husband Bilial found that funny. She continued, "In Pakistan, I had no choice. I had to wear a hijab. Here I have a choice." They were fascinating. Every group is made up of people with different and individual viewpoints.

Then Amira told me about the International House. I promised to go there with them. I liked getting to know people from different countries and cultures. Also, I could brush up on my Spanish in the classes offered there.

BILIAL (friend)

Amira's tenacity is frightening. That's how she got me to marry her. She wore me down. That's how I like to tell the story. Truly, she was the most impressive and beautiful woman I had ever met. Her soul and intelligence glowed through her face. As they say in America, I hit a home run when I married her.

But it is true that when she makes up her mind that something is going to happen—watch out! She will make it happen. She had decided that she is going to find Jamie Chen the right woman. I told her he just got to this country. He has just started on his Ph.D. He is young. He has plenty of time. But her reasoning had merit. We were even younger when we met and married. And having the right person—someone who is emotionally supportive—allows you to concentrate on your goals. It was true that we have helped and encouraged each other on our career paths. And we have companionship and fun together. That alone can free you to fulfill your purpose. Then Amira said what made the most sense to me. She said that most young people in this country have no one to help them—to look out for them—as we did when our parents introduced us. That is why there are so many mistakes and so many divorces. Amira has a good heart.

AMIRA (friend)

I called Jamie and invited him to meet us at the International House this Saturday. I said I had someone I wanted him to meet. Someone perfect for him. He asked what she was like. "Beautiful." That is always important to men. "Smart, tall, great personality."

Then I called Robin and asked her to come this Saturday to the International House to meet a young man. But she already had a date for Saturday. This caused me huge anxiety. I didn't want her to end up with the wrong person when I had the right person for her. She wanted to know his name. "Jamie Chen." And what was he like? "Handsome." Looks can matter to women too. "Smart, tall, great personality." Robin said she planned to study on Sunday but she could make it Sunday evening. I had to call Jamie back to tell him there was a change in plans. Could he make it Sunday evening? He said yes but he wanted to know her name. "Robin Dell." Okay, it was all arranged for Sunday evening at seven. Sometimes you get a feeling about people. I had that feeling.

ROBIN

David from my Insect Molecular Biology class kept asking me out. Maybe I was being closed-minded. I mean, I wasn't dating anyone I liked. In fact, I wasn't dating at all. And maybe it was unfair to hold his resemblance to my brother and his name against him. So I made a date with him for Saturday night.

Then Amira called to tell me she had someone interesting for me to meet on Saturday night. When I told her I already had plans, she suggested Sunday night instead. I had intended to study all day and night on Sunday but I didn't want to disappoint her. I asked what his name was. I thought she said James Cheney. I did find it a little difficult to understand her accented English on the phone. But I got enough information to be intrigued about this guy who Amira thought was perfect for me.

JAMIE

Amira said she had someone for me to meet on Saturday night. Then she called back to change the meeting to Sunday night. I admit that I was looking forward to meeting this Robin Dell. I hadn't had a special woman in my life since Lijuan. And I think most people hope they will have a meaningful connection with someone. Was this the right time for me? Who knows. So much in life is timing. Especially relationships.

I was studying on Saturday when Alicia called and suggested we go out for dinner that night. Good idea. She was pleasant company and I would like the break. We decided to have dinner at Paesanos.

ROBIN

David and I decided to have dinner at Paesanos. We had to wait 15 minutes before we could get a table. We filled the time with talk about the usual. Classes, our hometowns, families. Just getting to know each other. I kept looking at him. At how much he resembled my brother, Harry. As nice as David was, I just couldn't see myself with a boyfriend who looked like my brother.

When we were seated, he ordered a pizza and I ordered my favorite pasta dish, spaghetti olio. A woman walked by us. David recognized her. He got up and they hugged. He introduced the two of us, "Alicia this is Robin Dell. Robin, Alicia Mantel." David continued, "Alicia and I met while volunteering last summer at Cal Aggie Camp. It's an organization that helps underprivileged kids experience the outdoors." Wow. That sounded like a wonderful experience. Then Alicia's date caught up with her. I think my mouth fell open. It was the tall, good-looking Asian guy from my Quantitative Analysis class. Alicia introduced him. "Robin and David, this is Jamie Chen. Jamie, Robin Dell and David Richardson."

Jamie looked more than surprised at our introduction. Shocked was a better description. And then it hit me like a ton of bricks. Jamie Chen was Amira's "James Cheney." And Amira must have told him he was meeting Robin Dell on Sunday. This was awkward. Both of us realized we were going to have a blind date the next night. Except now we had met. Neither of us said anything. After all, we were on dates with other people.

While Alicia was explaining to Jamie how she knew David, Jamie and I were checking each other out. Trying to be subtle but probably not succeeding too well. Then Alicia suggested we all eat together. David turned the offer down by explaining our food was about to be delivered. I knew he wanted to spend alone time with me. And maybe he picked up on something strange passing between Jamie and me.

I tried to focus on David. And not show the edginess I felt. But thoughts kept running through my mind. Now I wanted to meet Jamie tomorrow. He was definitely appealing. But would he even be there? He was so cold to me before. How would I explain it to Amira and Bilial if he didn't show? Maybe I shouldn't show up. What if he 9blew me off again? I would feel terrible. But what plausible excuse could I give Amira? I could tell her I was sick. That sounded like the pathetic lie it would be. I could say I was afraid I would be hurt. That sounded even more pathetic. And I couldn't say I had accidentally met him and I wasn't interested. Another lie. I was interested.

I was facing toward their table but it was difficult to see them. There were lots of people at tables between us. But every now and then I saw him lean back in his chair and look our way. By the end of our dinner, I knew. I was going to the International House on Sunday evening. Whatever would happen—would happen.

JAMIE

I couldn't believe what just happened. Talk about chance. The girl from my Quantitative Analysis class. The girl from the bike rack meeting. The girl who seemed somehow familiar. The beautiful girl with auburn hair and green eyes. That was the girl who Amira was going to introduce me to tomorrow. I felt excited and fearful at the same time. What could Robin think of me? I had acted foolishly before. Maybe she wouldn't even bother to come. I would feel awful. I would have to explain everything to Amira and Bilial. Then I would feel even more foolish. But I really wanted to meet Robin. To have another chance to get to know her. And have her know me. A guy who *does* know how to say hello. In spite of my worries, I would be an honorable man. I would keep my promise to Amira. And my date with Robin.

ROBIN

By Sunday morning I was rethinking the meeting with Jamie. What if Amira's friend really was named James Cheney? What if Jamie Chen was just reacting to the awkward and unexpected way we had met at the bike rack, and not to my name? Should I call Amira to ask her more questions? Clearly, I was overthinking this and not getting much studying done. I decided to trust my gut. What I thought had happened had really happened. Just go, I told myself, and have a good time. Now all I had to do was decide what to wear.

AMIRA (friend)

Oh no! I had forgotten that Sunday was the International Festival at the International House. There was going to be lots of food from all over the world, culture booths, live entertainment. There would be lots of people. I wanted Jamie and Robin to be able to talk to each other. How would they be able to do that with all that craziness going on? I thought maybe I should call them and change the location or even change the date.

BILIAL (friend)

I told Amira to relax. All the activity could be good. It could take the pressure off them. And if they liked each other but they didn't like the commotion, they could choose to go somewhere else. We would get there early and wait inside the front door. That way neither of them had to look for us in all the chaos. She finally agreed with me.

JAMIE

I got to the International House about a quarter to seven. Amira and Bilial met me at the front door. The place was crowded with people enjoying the International Days Festival. Bilial was holding glasses of apple juice for me and for Robin. And then. There she was. I felt relief. This time I took her hand in my hands as I said, "Hi, Robin. It's good to see you again." Her smile was warm and sincere. She replied, "I've been looking forward to seeing you again too."

ROBIN

I found Amira and Bilial—and Jamie. He was genuinely friendly. I felt relief. Standing next to him, I realized he was two or three inches taller than me. Though I don't often wear high heels, it was nice to know I could wear them and not tower over him.

JAMIE

Amira was surprised that we seemed to know each other. But it was difficult to talk inside. Too noisy. Bilial suggested we sit at a table on the patio. As Bilial and I walked behind the women, I admired everything about Robin. From her pretty red dress, which complemented her lovely figure, to her shapely legs. She was wearing flats. I judged her to be about five foot ten. When I sat next to her, I again thought she was beautiful. And those amazing green eyes.

ROBIN

When we all sat down at an outside table, I explained to Amira and Bilial about our unexpected meeting Saturday night. They loved the story. It gave them a good laugh. The two of them are always laughing together. What a great quality to have in a relationship.

AMIRA (friend)

Jamie looked handsome in his khakis, untucked plaid shirt, sneakers and sweater around his shoulders. If I weren't married to the man I love! And Robin looked beautiful. The red color of her dress flattered her auburn hair and green eyes. They definitely were taken with each other. I was thrilled. I knew they would be perfect for each other. In fact, it didn't take long for Bilial and me to feel our presence was unnecessary. We decided to visit the booths to get some food. I don't think Robin and Jamie even noticed when we left the table.

JAMIE

I wanted to know everything about Robin. Where was she from? What were her parents like? Did she have sisters, brothers? Where did she get her undergraduate degree? What was she studying? What were her goals? She asked me a lot of questions too. We talked and talked. Sometimes it's like that. You just click with someone and the conversation is easy.

ROBIN

Amira and Bilial came back to the table with plates full of delicious food. Jamie suggested we get something to eat. When we got up, he took my hand. Honestly, I was impressed.

What young man does that today? Then, since it was getting cooler, he put his sweater around my shoulders. That was it! I was truly smitten.

At the food booths, I just took some vegetables. I was too excited to eat much. He chose a meat dish and some vegetables. I wouldn't have cared if he ate a whole cow. When we got back to the table, Amira and Bilial had finished eating and they made their escape. Jamie and I just kept talking. Then the festival ended. Everyone was breaking down their stands and leaving. Jamie again held my hand as he walked me back to my apartment. We exchanged cell numbers and made a date to sit together in our QA class. I wanted to kiss. I didn't know if we should kiss. We kissed. It was all good.

JAMIE

I liked many things about Robin. I found her to be intelligent and attractive. But there was more than that. We had a lot in common. My father had died and I wanted to research cures for cancer. Her mother had MS and she wanted to find a cure for that disease. The environment was important to both of us. We both were close to our families. We both loved nature. We both admired Amira and Bilial's relationship. Especially their ability to laugh at themselves. So there we were. Robin and I. From two different worlds and so much the same. It was easy to relate to her. To talk to her.

ROBIN

I was fully in the excitement—really the thrill—of emotional happiness. Now I knew what the expression "walking on air" meant. And when I saw Annie/Frannie the next day at the

Viridian gym, my joy was obvious to them. Annie asked, "What's going on with you? You look so happy. You're glowing. Did you have sex or fall in love?"

I answered, "The latter!" They wanted to know everything. I excitedly told them the whole story.

Then Annie said, "You have only been here a couple of months. You just met him. What do you really know about him? What if you got married? Where would you live? China?"

Deflated! It was easy to sow doubt. Easy to bring me down. But Frannie surprised me with her question, "What will your parents think about him being Chinese?" With that question, all my uncertainty disappeared. I knew my parents. I knew they would love Jamie.

🍃   🍃   🍃

JAMIE

I couldn't believe my strong attraction to Robin. My feelings were sudden and unexpected. I had seen movies where people fall in love immediately. Did that really happen? Was it love that I was feeling?

JAKE (friend)

Jamie called me. He wanted to tell me about a girl he had met. I could tell he needed to talk. I told him to come over to my place. When he got here—he *really* needed to talk. He told me the whole story in detail. How they had sort of met—but not really. And the surprising introduction at Paesanos. And then the evening at the International House. I had never heard Jamie buzz so much.

When he finished talking he asked what I thought. Could someone fall in love that fast? Was he rushing into something? How does a guy know when someone is right for them? I said, "Getting a degree. Getting a job. Those are the easy things. Finding someone you want to be with, someone to love and to love you. That's hard." And hey, I'm from California. I told him to relax and enjoy himself. "Don't overthink it. Go with the flow."

🍃 🍃 🍃

ROBIN

Jamie and I had made plans to meet before our QA class on Tuesday. But he called me Monday evening to see if I wanted to study together. I did. We met at the library. After we sat across from each other and opened our books, it was obvious that neither of us could concentrate. We gave up on studying and went to a coffee shop where we could talk. We didn't run out of subjects. I found him fascinating. He told me about Guilin and China. About how he experienced America. About his mother and her business. About his classes. About his love for plants. And here was the rare guy who was interested in what I had to say. He listened and asked me lots of questions.

JAMIE

As we spent more and more time together, it was clear to us that we had to get back to studying. We both had papers we had to write. And midterm exams were coming up. Studying at each other's apartments was not going to work. We went to the library and used adjoining study desks. But we would hold hands and talk around the partitions. We laughed at how ineffective that was. We finally used study desks in separate areas. That worked better.

ROBIN

We got our papers done and finished midterms. Thanksgiving was up next. I was going home. Jamie wasn't going back to China until winter break. Now things were getting tricky. Even though Thanksgiving wasn't a familiar holiday for him, the campus would be deserted. I didn't want him to be alone. But if I invited him to join me in Sherburne, was I rushing things? Meeting my parents already! And even though my parents thought I could be impulsive, would they think it was weird if I brought home a boyfriend I had only known a month? My dilemma was solved when Jake invited Jamie to his home in Los Angeles—actually Brentwood—for Thanksgiving. Jamie was excited to be driving along the coast. Seeing Big Sur. Seeing Los Angeles. Though I couldn't wait to see my family, I felt a little jealous. I would have loved seeing Big Sur with Jamie. Maybe another time.

AMIRA (friend)

Robin kept me informed about her relationship with Jamie. Of course I was delighted. I missed my true calling. I should have studied psychology. I understand people.

6

HOMES AT LAST

Sherburne, Vermont

ROBIN

It was great to see my parents, and even Harry. Everyone was doing well. Including Mom. A new medication she was taking had resulted in some improvement. She was able to walk using her cane more often.

During the plane ride home, I considered how I would tell Mom and Dad about Jamie. I decided I would wait a while before I casually mentioned him. However, I don't have a poker face. What I am feeling is my expression. And when Mom and Dad said I looked happy—even radiant—I blurted out the whole story. Thankfully, Harry wasn't around to tease me. They said they were happy to hear that I had a special "friend" in my life but they had a lot of questions. Was this too sudden? Did I think this was serious? Were we moving too fast? What about my studies? My goals? What about his goals? Then they asked what was really on their minds. If this led to marriage, where would we live? China?

MAGGIE (Mom)

When Robbie told us she met someone she really liked, I was surprised. Bobby and I always thought Robbie would some-day find someone special. But this seemed rather sudden. Maybe too sudden. She had only been gone a few months. And sometimes she did act impulsively. But as parents, we could only caution her to take her time. To make sure this is the right person. If we pushed her to break it off, she might blame us for a long time. Then Robbie showed us a selfie of her with Jamie. He certainly was handsome. And they did look especially joyful together. Truly ecstatic. I wondered how Jamie's mother would react. Would she accept Robbie? Or would she try to influence him to end the relationship? Maybe find a Chinese girl?

BOBBY (Dad)

And here we thought our worst fear was that Robbie would end up living on the West Coast. Now our fear was that she would live in China. That was just too far away. When I brought up that possibility, she said they weren't discussing marriage—let alone where they live. What could we do? We had to remain cool. By Christmas their relationship could be over.

AUNT SUE (Maggie's sister)

As always, I was looking forward to Thanksgiving with the family. Thanksgiving and Christmas in Vermont are like living in a Norman Rockwell painting. And I was excited to see the kids. Particularly since Robbie was home from school. She looked great. I figured her glow was caused by all that California sunshine. Then she confided her spark was due to a new boyfriend. That was unexpected but these things do happen. Anyway, I was delighted for her.

Then we all got another jolt at Thanksgiving dinner when Harry announced he had met someone he was serious about. Her name was Helen and she was in her medical residency. In gynecology. A handy expertise for any future pregnancy. And an easy decision for a wedding gift. Monogrammed "H & H" towels. Robbie was happy for him. And relieved. The attention was off her. But I couldn't tell if Maggie and Bobby were thrilled or shell-shocked.

ROBIN

Between my revelation about Jamie and Harry's announcement about Helen, the family clearly had an exciting Thanksgiving. Getting together with Julie was a reprieve. She was her usual calm and accepting self. When I told her that Harry was going to bring Helen home for Christmas, she asked if I was going to bring Jamie. Now that's a thought.

Los Angeles, California

JAMIE

I was glad that Jake invited me to Los Angeles for Thanksgiving. Since I knew I would miss Robin, I needed a distraction. And the trip was a good experience. We drove down to L.A. on U.S. 101. An inland but quicker route. Lots and lots of farmland. Rolling hills at first. Then flattening out. Then more mountains as we approached Southern California. I liked Los Angeles. Very spread out. The areas I saw—Brentwood, Bel Air, Beverly Hills, Santa Monica—were beautiful with many more trees than I expected. The trees were welcoming to me and so were Jake's parents, Ben and Susan. Before the holiday feast, they took me for lunch at a Santa Monica hotel, Shutters. Our table overlooked the incredibly wide beach. Then we went to the pier to ride the Ferris wheel. Seeing the ocean from that perspective was fun.

The next day I experienced my first Thanksgiving dinner. And just like popular holidays in other countries, the emphasis on family and good food is a winning combination. Still, I felt a little lonely for my own family. Instead of my daily text to Mother, I called her. It was good to hear her voice. During our conversation, I told her I had met a girl I really liked. She didn't seem surprised. But she surprised me by not asking if she was Chinese.

LING (Mother)

While Jinsong was on his Thanksgiving vacation, he unexpectedly called me. Usually he texted during the week and called on the weekend. He sounded happy. That always made me feel good. He said he wanted to wish me a cheerful Thanksgiving. I knew he was joking since it is not a Chinese holiday. He was in Los Angeles at a friend's house. I was thankful Jamie had made such a good friend. He described his trip to Los Angeles and the city and the Thanksgiving dinner.

I could tell that something else was on his mind. I was patient. Finally he told me. He had met a girl he really liked. I thought to myself that this girl must be special. Otherwise he would not have talked about her. I did not ask if she was Chinese. I think most mothers would want to know the girl's ethnicity but it wasn't important to me. I did not want him to feel pressure from me. His happiness with the right young woman was what I cared about. I also wasn't concerned he had found someone quickly. I knew my son. He was a responsible young man.

Pacific Coast Highway 1

JAMIE

Jake took the scenic route back to Davis. We drove along the ocean. Through Malibu, Santa Barbara, San Simeon, Big Sur, Carmel and Monterey. Then we went east to connect with U.S. 101. Of all these areas, Big Sur was my favorite. So beautiful. The forested mountains descending to the wild and exciting ocean. The natural world felt close and personal.

While driving through Big Sur, we stopped to eat at Nepenthe, a restaurant overlooking the ocean. Suddenly I was overwhelmed by the chatter from trees. I didn't realize how good I had gotten at blocking out their conversation. Now I was relaxed and I heard them loudly. Or maybe it was the setting. Even the trees were happy there. I wished Robin was with me. I missed her. I made a mental note to take her to this special place.

Davis, California

ROBIN

It was good to be with my family for Thanksgiving. But I must admit I couldn't wait to see Jamie. Was this how love felt? It had to be.

JAMIE

I called Robin on my way back to Davis. We made a date for later that evening. I felt an anxiousness I knew would not go away until I saw her. And when we were together, I experienced a great sense of relief and joy. She was just as happy to see me.

ROBIN

We didn't want to be apart again. Sometimes I would stay at Jamie's apartment. But most of the time he stayed at my place. Not only was it bigger than his apartment but it came with benefits he liked. A pool and a gym. We decided that at the end of the fall quarter exams—after the second week in December—he would give up his place and move in with me.

JAMIE

We made a plan for winter break. We would go to Vermont for the first week so Robin could be there for Christmas Eve. Then on Christmas Day, we would fly to China to be with my mother. It was a lot of flying but we wanted to meet each other's families. I hoped Robin's parents would like me. She was confident they would. I knew my mother would like her.

ROBIN

Amira was right. Being together made life easier. We encouraged each other to concentrate on our studies. We were working on a future together. But we hadn't gone through the "meet the parents" experience. We knew the questions that would be asked. Are you planning on getting married? When? Where will you live? How do you plan to pursue your respective careers? We asked ourselves the same questions. We knew we were right for each other. Yes, we thought we would eventually get married. But we didn't have any specific plan or time. We would live in America. Probably on the West Coast because it was sort of halfway between both families. Exactly where would depend on being able to get positions in our respective fields in the same city.

🍃 🍃 🍃

MAGGIE (Mom)
On their winter break, Robin and Jamie first came to Vermont. Bobby and I felt much better after we met Jamie. His maturity, his warmth, his love and care for Robin. We were impressed. We could see why Robin loved him. But we were relieved they weren't rushing into marriage. We also met Harry's girlfriend. A lovely young woman. We liked her too. We thought she was "good" for Harry.

ROBIN
I liked Helen, Harry's fiancée. She was so smart that I wondered what she was doing with my brother! They wanted to have a summer wedding. Probably in June.

MAGGIE (Mom)
Harry and Helen were both living in Boston. He was finishing his doctorate in environmental engineering and she was finishing her residency at Massachusetts General. Her family was from Brookline. A Boston suburb. Their wedding would be in the Boston area. And in addition to phone conversations,

Helen's parents planned a trip to Vermont in April to meet Bobby and me in person. That was kind of them.

ROBIN

Since Jamie's mother was going to be in San Francisco in the spring with her travel friends, Mom and Dad said they would consider making a trip to San Francisco to meet her. I was touched by their thoughtfulness. And though they didn't verbalize it, I knew their plans would depend on whether Jamie and I continued our serious relationship.

BOBBY (Dad)

Wow! One wedding coming up and maybe another one sooner or later. Maggie and I talked it over before telling Robbie and Jamie we would consider flying to San Francisco in March to meet Jamie's mother. Flying can be difficult for Maggie but—assuming they were still a committed couple— she insisted she wanted to do it. We just wanted everything to start off right for them.

We thought Jamie was delightful. He was smart and funny. He obviously loved Robbie. Lighting up whenever he was with her. But the most important thing to me was that he treated Robin with respect and consideration. And we really liked Helen. We felt fortunate our children had found such exceptional people.

Guilin, China

ROBIN

On Christmas Day we left to go halfway round the world to see Ling, Jamie's mother. It was hard to leave my family. I would have normally spent the whole winter break with them. But I realized it's what couples do when they want to spend time with each faraway family. We flew through Beijing on our way to Guilin. Maybe another time Jamie would show me the city. Now we wanted to get to Guilin to spend as much time as possible with Ling.

I was surprised when I met her. She was young-looking. She said her beautiful skin was the result of her own creams. I definitely wanted to load up with her products. And I loved Ling. She was warm and wise and funny and smart. There was also something about her. I don't know—she was perceptive.

JAMIE

Robin had started taking Mandarin lessons at the International House. And to my surprise, Mother had begun taking English lessons. But mostly I had to interpret for them. They promised each other they would be more fluent in each other's languages by the end of March when we would meet in San Francisco.

ROBIN

Jamie took me to see the farmhouse where he spent his early years and the "special" pine tree he was named after. What a lovely setting. He actually hugged the pine tree. He said the tree told him I was the right girl for him. What a sense of humor!

JAMIE

Good thing Robin and I are young. Otherwise I don't think we could have handled all the flying we did in just over two weeks. But it was worth it. Seeing where Robin grew up. Meeting her family. They were wonderful. I was impressed with everyone and everything. Especially how comfortable and accepted they made me feel. To find a special woman I loved and get a great new family. I was a lucky man.

LING (Mother)

How could I not love Robin? She was everything Jinsong described. A lovely young woman. Clever and amusing and sincere. And if they had children, they surely would grow tall. But the most important thing is that she clearly loved my Jinsong. Would I have preferred he had found a Chinese girl? It probably would have meant he would live in China but not likely in Guilin anyway. As long as he was happy. That is what mattered to me.

One strange thing did happen during the visit. I complained about the termites in my house. I felt embarrassed about the bugs. However, I knew Robin was studying insects and I wanted her advice. She simply said not to worry. The termites would leave. And they did. I never saw another one. She was going to be a great entomologist!

California

ROBIN

Jamie and I fell into a routine. We studied harder than ever. We were working toward a mutual goal. We'd go swimming or exercise several evenings during the week. We'd get together with friends on weekends. Amira and Bilial, Jake, Annie/Frannie. Jake and Annie started dating. I guess they had the California vibe in common. And with Jamie's help and lessons at the International House, my Mandarin was improving.

Jamie loved Big Sur. He wanted to take me there. And I wanted to see Carmel, Blair's hometown. When President's Day in February gave us a three-day weekend, we decided to rent a car and drive down to Carmel and Big Sur.

JAMIE

We walked around Carmel first. A charming town on the ocean. A beautiful sunny day. We could imagine living there. Until a store clerk told us how rare the sunshine was—especially in the winter. She said Carmel is often fogged in.

We stayed in Big Sur. At a place called Deetjen's Big Sur Inn. It was reasonable and had lots of rustic charm. We couldn't have imagined a more perfect place. The next day, as we hiked the redwood forest, I heard the trees talking. They were talking to me. Louder and louder. "She's the one. She's the one." At last, I found a fallen tree and asked Robin to sit down. I was nervous. I knew the time had come for me to tell her about my ability to communicate with plants. Especially with trees. What would she think? That I was crazy? Delusional? Would she still want to be with me?

ROBIN

Our weekend trip was romantic. I didn't think it was possible to feel even more in love than I already did. I never expected to feel so special, so valued. But when we were hiking, he became tense. He said he needed to tell me something. We sat down on a log. Negative thoughts rushed to my mind. Was he ill? Did he take me on this beautiful trip just to break up with me? Did I do something wrong? Then Jamie told me, "I can communicate with trees and plants. And I can influence their activities." I couldn't hold back my tears.

JAMIE

Robin started crying. This was it. It was over. Then she revealed to me, "I can communicate with insects. I can control their behavior. I didn't know how to tell you. I feared you would think I was crazy and reject me." Suddenly I realized why all the termites had disappeared from my mother's house. My relief was so strong. I felt as though my happiness would burst through my heart. We believed each other because we both had these strange abilities. Gifts really.

ROBIN

My tears came from a sense of release. I was not alone. We could tell each other who we really were. Be who we really were. Everything immediately made sense to me. Our attraction was more than emotional and physical. It was also metaphysical.

JAMIE

Robin asked me, "What are the trees saying?" I answered, "They've been telling me that you're the one." Then I found a plant stem on the forest floor and wound it into a small circle. I got down on one knee and asked her to marry me. I had never felt more certain about anything in my whole life.

ROBIN

My response? Yes! I wanted to know if the ring made from a stem was telling him anything. He put it to his ear and said, "It told me to get you a proper ring." I think he made that up but he wouldn't admit it.

JAMIE

During our drive home, my excitement and happiness were tempered by a nagging thought I couldn't dismiss. Now that Robin and I had disclosed our most personal secrets, I wanted to know more about her power with insects. I knew it was a little childish and insecure. I couldn't help myself. Was her ability more powerful and important than mine? I questioned her.

"Robin, have you ever used your ability to control insects for anything—like anything important?"

She laughed. "Do you count the times I let mosquitos bite my brother? Or the times I impressed my friend Julie by having bees fly in the direction she picked? What do you consider important?"

I mean using your power in a way that helps people or animals. You know. Something important."

"I guess you wouldn't count the time I made the termites leave your mother's house as important?"

"No. That was nice and helpful but I meant "lifesaving" important."

"I did tell you about the time I was hiking. How Julie and I had to fight off a man who tried to attack us."

"Yes, I remember that. You two were really brave."

"But what I didn't tell you is how I finally overcame him."

"I thought you and Julie jumped on him and disarmed him. What else happened?"

"It is true that after we wrestled him to the ground I was able to grab his gun. But he got up and ran into the woods. We followed him because then I had the gun and he was headed toward where my dog, Waldo, was barking. When we caught up to him, the guy was holding Waldo. He threatened to smash him against a tree if I didn't give him his gun."

"Did you shoot him?"

"I had never fired a gun. I was afraid I would hit Waldo. I stalled for time while I called on every ant in the area to attack him. Within just a few minutes, hundreds and hundreds of ants crawled all over him. They went up his pant legs, under his jacket, on his face, in his hair. They also bit him. He had to drop Waldo while he slapped at the ants on his body. And in desperation he peeled off his pants and ran away into the woods."

I was quiet for a few minutes while I thought about Robin's impressive use of insects. Then she broke the silence.

"I didn't tell you this before because I didn't know how to tell you about my unique relationship with insects. I was afraid you would think I wasn't sane."

"That's not what I was thinking about. I was thinking my ability to communicate and control trees and plants is a magic trick compared to your gift with insects."

"How have you used your power?"

"I used it to help rice plants grow. And to help my mother find the herbs she needed. Things like that. Oh, and once I asked trees to direct me to the two guys who had stolen the Kindles' dog, Bao Wao. I know I told you about that. But I left out the part about the trees giving me directions for the same reason you left the ants out of your story."

"I remember you telling me about Bao Wao's dognapping. That was amazing! You saved a dog's life and the broken hearts of the Kindle children. And trees aided you. It's true I rescued Waldo at Camel's Hump. But when he was dying, I was unable to do anything for him. I desperately wanted to save him. At least until I got home from Costa Rico. Would trees have been able to help me?"

"It's possible. Trees are remarkably wise. They may have told you about a plant that could have helped Waldo."

I could see the wheels turning in Robin's head. The regret we all feel when we wish we could do something over. Make the outcome different.

I said, "Robin, the point is your control over insects seems to have a direct correlation to changing a situation. I don't know how I can use my power with plants to really make a difference. In an important lifesaving way."

"Didn't you just say that trees are truly wise? That they and other plants have directed you to healing herbs? That they told you how to find the guys who took Bao Wao? I don't know exactly how either of us will use our powers to help people or animals or plants. But we must trust that we have these abilities for a reason. They are not just for amusement. We will discover our purpose. I'm sure of it."

I felt myself relax. My mind was clearer. I was going to marry a smart woman. I knew it wouldn't be my only time of self-doubt but I also knew Robin would be there to encourage me. To help me through those difficult periods. We would help each other.

🍃 🍃 🍃

ROBIN

We decided we wanted to get married in the summer. We picked July 3. That worked for a lot of reasons. Since our wedding would be in Sherburne, we'd already be back on the East Coast for Harry and Helen's June wedding. Harry and Helen would be back from their honeymoon by then. And family and friends would likely have that weekend free.

JAMIE

Our honeymoon plan was to volunteer at the Cal Aggie Camp. An outdoor experience for inner-city and underprivileged kids. After we heard David and Alicia describe their experience at the camp, we really wanted to participate. It also seemed appropriate because the camp was indirectly—by way of David and Alicia—responsible for our first formal introduction.

MAGGIE (Mom)

This was very exciting! Two weddings in one summer. Bobby and I were given the assignment of making the plans and arrangements for Robin and Jamie's wedding. Thank goodness, Harry and Helen's wedding was being handled by Helen and her mother.

Robin was never one to fantasize about a big wedding and a fancy gown. She gave me some instructions. Outside on the lawn of our house. Not formal. All-denominational. Vegetarian food provided for the vegetarians. And she wanted to wear my wedding dress. A simple long, off-white silk slip dress. That made me cry. I never considered myself a managing mother but this was my chance to make my daughter's wedding what I wanted it to be. Special and surprising.

BOBBY (Dad)

Maggie and I decided on an evening wedding with torches lining the aisle. The dinner was served in an open-sided tent. Everything was done in white. White slip-covered chairs, tablecloths and candles. The table centerpieces were made of living greens with fragrant pine needles arranged around white candles. I have to admit. It all reflected Maggie's elegant style.

Robin insisted that no bug deterrent devices would be necessary. I thought, she knows bugs better than we do. Perhaps candles and aromatic green arrangements kept insects away. I sure hoped so.

MAGGIE (Mom)

Even though it was Fourth of July weekend, we couldn't have fireworks. Private displays are not permitted in Vermont. However, I had an alternative idea up my sleeve.

I was determined to walk down the aisle so we put down a temporary hardwood walkway. But rather than escort Robbie, I decided to walk with Jamie. Our new son. I felt I would be standing in for his mother. And though I realized having both parents walk their child down the aisle gave the mother as important a role as the father, it looked a little overwhelming to me. As if the parents had to make sure their child couldn't escape. So Bobby alone, symbolically, did the politically incorrect act of giving his daughter to another man.

BOBBY (Dad)

In March we traveled to San Francisco to meet Jamie's mother Ling. And to be with Jamie and Robbie. It went well. We liked Ling. She was impressive. A self-made successful woman. We could see many of her traits in Jamie. His interest in other people, his thoughtfulness, his directness, his sense of humor.

MAGGIE (Mom)

Ling was expanding her line internationally. She and her sister, Jamie's Auntie Mei, would be in Europe for business meetings at the time of the Sherburne wedding. But the kids had already decided to have another wedding in China in August. That way they could spend the month with her.

Before everyone returned home, Robin and Jamie took Ling, Bobby and me on a day trip to Davis to see the campus, the town, their apartment. We even had a pizza at their favorite restaurant, Paesanos. Understanding where Robbie and Jamie's life was happening helped us feel a part of their experience.

Sherburne, Vermont

ROBIN

The rest of the school year went by quickly. All of a sudden we were in Boston for Harry and Helen's wedding. Then up to Vermont for the remainder of June before our wedding.

With summer weather, I exposed Jamie to all my passions. Beehives, hiking in the Adirondacks, sailing on Lake Champlain. And he met my friends.

Blair, Julie and Brianna were my bridesmaids. What an anti-
quated term. "Maids." Short for "maidens." I liked "support
team" better. We also wanted Amira and Bilial to be part of our
wedding party. I was afraid their Muslim faith would prevent
them from participating. But Bilial said, "No problem." They
belonged to the Progressive Muslim Union and there weren't
such restrictions in the movement's interpretation of the Koran.

JAMIE

The Kindles, my American family in Beijing, were back living
in the U.S. The whole family came to our wedding. It was
wonderful to see them again, especially the kids. They were
now 19, 17 and 13. Jerry Kindle, Bilial, Jake and Harry "stood
up" for me. Everybody needs someone standing up for them
in this life.

ROBIN

I am taller than Mom so her wedding dress was tea length
on me. I liked it even better that way. No veil but I wore my
hair in a loose and tousled up-do with two white azaleas from
our garden woven in. When I saw the look on Jamie's face,
I felt beautiful.

BLAIR (friend)

It was fun to finally meet everyone who was special in Robin's
life. We women—Amira, Julie, Brianna and I—organized what
we would wear. We decided to get different dresses we each
personally liked and would be comfortable wearing. But all
the dresses would be some shade of green. That was to
honor Jamie and Robin's commitment to the environment.

Robin's friend, Brianna, designed and made her own dress. It was a stunning off-the-shoulder mid-length sheath that complemented her perfectly. The men in the wedding wore dark suits accented with green ties. And Jamie had a white azalea in his lapel. Robin told me later that when she saw him—he was so handsome—her heart skipped a beat.

ROBIN

Jamie and I wrote our vows together. It was the same vow for both of us. Short and sweet. "We will love, value and respect each other. We will put each other's happiness first. Though we are individuals, our marriage symbolizes our entwining as one." Mom's best friend, Alice, a Unitarian minister, officiated. And after the brief ceremony, all the guests—about 100 people—formed a circle around us and lit sparklers. It was Mom's surprise. The only bugs that were invited were fireflies. Lots of them. That was my secret surprise.

I never daydreamed about my marriage ceremony. So it was a joy that Mom and Dad made it what they wanted. They planned a wonderful wedding. Jamie and I thought it was beautiful and perfect.

JULIE (friend)

I think every single woman who attends a wedding, especially a best friend's wedding, hopes to find the same love and happiness. I know that's how I felt that magical evening. And then I caught the bouquet!

California

JAMIE

After Vermont, we flew back to Davis to volunteer as counselors at the Cal Aggie Camp. Besides the usual camp experiences—swimming in the lake, campfires and sing-alongs—I taught the kids some kung fu moves and Chinese words. "Ni hao" for hello. "Xie xie" for thank you. Phonetically "nee how" and "syeh syeh." Words like that. And Robin shared interesting facts about insects' lives. One of the kids, Jasmine, made me a friendship bracelet that I still wear. It was such a rewarding and fun experience. Neither Robin nor I could have wished for a better honeymoon.

We followed that week up with a few days in the Sequoia National Forest. Robin wanted me to experience the giant Sequoia trees. We both wanted to know if these trees, many over 2,000 years old, had any special information. They did. They told me we were a special couple. Our life together was going to extend in a singular direction. And we would have a major impact on the natural world. That was an exciting prediction for us. But also a troubling feeling of the unknown. Of responsibility. For what?

ROBIN

As we were hiking we studied the trail map. We could see that there was a shortcut back to where we were staying.

Wuksachi Lodge. We just had to go up the hill and hook up with the trail at the top. It was getting late. That could save us time. And we would experience a new trail and scenery with, hopefully, fewer hikers. We started up the hill. But the crest wasn't a short way up. Once we got to what appeared from below to be the top, there was a new summit to reach. It was a difficult ascent. The dirt was soft. We had to traverse the hill in a zigzag pattern. Every time we got to what had looked like the pinnacle, we found we had to climb more. But we were committed. We kept going.

After a half hour, we finally reached the ridge. But the return trail was nowhere to be seen. The area was deserted. We saw a faint path just wide enough for one person. Feeling confident it would eventually overlap the main trail, we marched on. I walked in front of Jamie. We saw bear excrement. That made us nervous. We hoped we wouldn't come across a mother bear with her cub.

JAMIE

It was a peaceful and pleasant walk. Then—unexpectedly piercing the quiet—we heard high-pitched howls interspersed with a snarling growl. We knew immediately. An animal was in trouble. And it was in pain. Without hesitation Robin took off. She was fast. I remembered she had run track in high school. I ran after her. She saw the terrible scene first.

ROBIN

As I got within sight of the wailing animal, I saw a man who had somehow captured a coyote. That was definitely against the law. But worse yet, the man was beating the poor animal with a thick branch while it was entrapped in a net.

JAMIE

Robin ran toward the man as she yelled, "Stop it! Stop it!" The man swung the branch around and hit her in the head. She went down. I swear my heart stopped. All I could think of was Robin. She wasn't moving. Her eyes were closed. Was she alive?

I ran up to her and knelt beside her just before the guy swung at me. Was it the movement of air from his swing or did a tree warn me? I dove to one side but the branch hit my shoulder. My adrenalin was pumping. I didn't feel anything. When he swung again, I grabbed the end of the branch and pulled it out of his hand. He drew a large knife from a scabbard tied to his leg. If he was going to use it to skin the coyote, he now was going to skin me. I caught one of his legs with a scissor-leg hold and tripped him. He fell backward. I jumped up and so did he.

Now we faced each other. Except he still had that knife. He was a big guy. Maybe six foot, three. Slicked-back dark hair and a big black beard. And he was quick. He swung the knife at me. I was quick too. I jumped away from his lunges. I assumed a fighting stance. Basically a boxing position with one foot slightly in front of the other and my fists up. I blocked his next thrust by checking his arm with my right arm and hitting him with my left. As he stumbled backward, I used a stomp kick. Bringing my right foot out in front of my bent right leg and then snapping it forward. That sent him shooting away from me. I leaped forward and made a grab for the knife by digging my fingers into the tendons of his forearm. He dropped it but he jammed his knee into my chest. The air went out of me. This time I staggered backward. He threw his weight against me and we both ended up sprawled on the ground. Only he was on top of me. He threw a punch but I twisted my body. His blow again caught my shoulder. I ignored the pain and pushed him off me as I caught him with a jab to his jaw.

Suddenly a swarm of wasps flew in and attacked the man. Repeatedly stinging his head. He screamed in pain as he hobbled to his feet. Flailing his arms, he tried frantically to protect his face only to have his hands stung. He ran. Trying to outrun the wasps. My last sight of him was the back of his head and neck—already turning red, lumpy and swollen.

I looked over at Robin. She was sitting up. I instantly realized she had called the wasps to attack him. I felt tremendous relief that she was okay. I hugged and kissed her. Then helped her to her feet. She was bleeding from a gash on the side of her head and was woozy. I suspected she had a concussion. But her first concern was for me. My shoulder was swelling fast. She thought it was broken.

ROBIN

We used the guy's knife to cut the net and free the coyote. It ran off. Then we supported each other as we found our way to the main trail leading back to the lodge. A staff member helped bandage my head and gave Jamie ice packs for his shoulder. We were some banged-up pair.

JAMIE

It was a sleepless, uncomfortable night for both of us. Robin had a headache and bouts of dizziness. My shoulder was swollen and bruised. And it hurt. During this restless period, I thought a lot about what had happened. Robin's independence and boldness made it impossible for me to prevent her from getting hurt. I would have to help her be more careful, more cautious. I vowed to myself to do a better job of protecting her.

It was a relief when dawn finally arrived. We drove down the mountain to the Kaweah Delta Medical Center in Visalia. Both of our fears—Robin's concussion and my fractured shoulder—proved true.

ROBIN

The only other time I had used insects to attack someone was when I saved Waldo. I used ants then. Maybe harmless but, in massive numbers, extremely irritating and painful. In Sequoia my only thought was to help Jamie. I needed fast results and wasps did the trick. I hoped I would never have to use insects that way again.

Guilin, China

JAMIE

By August we were healed enough to travel to China for another wedding and a pleasurable time with my mother. Robin's concussion symptoms had receded. I had to wear a sling for two more weeks. As Robin had done with her parents, I let Mother plan the wedding.

On the long plane ride to China, I reflected on our life together. Everything was good and right for us. We were truly fortunate. Having each other, having great families, having exciting career directions. Even though I was not superstitious, I couldn't help but to feel uneasy about our good fortune. If there is providence—will it balance things out?

ROBIN

Our Chinese wedding was on the 18th of August. An auspicious date for weddings in China. Ling and I had fun shopping for a wedding dress. We selected a pretty dress that was more traditionally bridal than my Sherburne wedding dress. Long lace sleeves and bodice, a full skirt and a veil. Since I was not wearing the traditional Chinese red gown, we found a pair of red fabric shoes with embroidered dragons and mandarin ducks. A bird that mates for life. The wedding outfit search—and being more conversant in each other's language—helped us bond even more.

JAMIE

Our wedding, as with many Chinese weddings, was mostly Western-style. It was held at the Shangri-La Hotel on a park-like lawn bordering the Li River. The city of Guilin and the mountains were a beautiful backdrop across the river. The ceremony started in the morning at 28 minutes after ten. Again, the lucky number eight. Robin was escorted by my Uncle Zihao to a pretty Chinese-style gazebo surrounded by guests seated on yellow-covered chairs.

Like most people in China, my family didn't practice a clergy-organized religion. We had the wedding planner, Mr. Deng, preside as we exchanged vows. The same ones we pledged in Vermont. My high school friends—Liang, Bai and Jiang—were my best men. Two of my aunts and my only female cousin were Robin's best women.

ROBIN

After the ceremony, everyone went inside to an elegant banquet hall with fabric-covered panels alternating with mirrors and painted scenes of the Guilin mountains. A dozen amazing crystal chandeliers hung from the 30-foot ceiling. The chairs and tables were covered in red damask fabric. The red and white floral arrangements were in tall fluted vases.

There were at least 300 guests. The Chen extended family, Ling's friends and their families, Jamie's friends and their families, Ling's employees and their families. Everyone Ling and Jamie knew or had ever known.

JAMIE

Mother had ordered a sumptuous banquet. The menu was 12 courses. Lobster, shrimp, braised beef, pork ribs, egg rolls, Peking duck, all kinds of filled dumplings, jellyfish, century eggs, gong bao chicken, wonton soup, dragon beard candy and my favorite treat, almond cookies.

ROBIN

Before the meal there was wonderful entertainment. Traditional Chinese singers and dancers. I was thrilled and touched by the beautiful songs and dances. The lion dancers were so colorful and awesome.

JAMIE

We included traditional Chinese customs. One was the new pair of shoes Robin wore. Another was that Robin and I linked arms and drank from each other's goblets. Often this is done in a private ceremony. However, since the glasses were tied together with a red ribbon, we choose to amuse our guests with this tricky maneuver. This act is symbolic of our first difficulty to overcome. Also of our never-ending union. And when the soup was served, we went from table to table toasting our guests. That resulted in a lot of drinking for us!

ROBIN

Everyone was friendly and gracious. As the guests left, Jamie and Ling and I stood at the door of the banquet hall to thank everyone for coming. I think a good time was had by all. I know Jamie and I had a wonderful time. And sharing this special occasion with Ling was our greatest happiness.

Again, I found myself marveling at Ling. She was smart. And capable. But she wasn't a mother who was trying to live through her child. She had made a meaningful life for herself. If Jamie was happy, she was happy. She knew I felt the same way.

JAMIE

Before we left Guilin, Robin and I visited the pine tree at the farmhouse. This time we both hugged the tree. The tree told me we would be back someday.

LING (Mother)

Having a wedding for Jinsong and Robin was a great pleasure for me. Having them spend a month with me was truly special. I felt a part of their love and happiness. Jamie was Chinese and Robin was American. But they were well matched. They seemed somehow to be the same.

JAMIE

In China, a woman doesn't take her husband's surname. And in America, a woman sometimes keeps her own surname or uses a hyphenated name. Robin said she wanted to use "Robin Chen-Dell. I said then I would use "Jamie Dell-Chen." That gave her a good laugh. She said she couldn't see introducing us as Ms. Chen-Dell and Mr. Dell-Chen. Imagine the confusion. So I stuck with Jamie Jinsong Chen. Or maybe I will be Chen-Dell too. We'll see.

7

GRADUATING
TO THE UNKNOWN

California

JAMIE

In graduate school the classes are smaller and harder. Especially in your discipline. There are many more seminar classes where a student's presentation leads to a lively discussion. These courses certainly teach a person to think critically and analytically. We enjoyed the lab classes the most. They allowed us to sharpen our research skills. And we were each able to connect with professors who eventually hired us as research assistants. That was one way to earn a stipend from a university.

ROBIN

As our studies continued we began to realize that we were both working on the same problem—but different sides of the same coin. Jamie wanted to find what could stimulate the immune system to fight off and kill cancer cells. I wanted to find what causes an immune system to become over-stimu-lated, possibly resulting in diseases such as multiple sclerosis. What if the answer was the same for both problems?

JAMIE

After two more years of coursework, it came time to take our comprehensive exams in our respective fields. We cut short our usual visits to my mother and to Robin's parents so we could study, study, study. We both passed.

ROBIN

What an ordeal. We needed a break. Some fun. We visited Amira and Bilial. They were living and working in Silicon Valley. Amira worked for a research center in Cupertino. Bilial for an online sales company in Sunnyvale. And they were expecting their first child. It was wonderful to share in their joy. But I did feel a pang of envy. I envisioned Jamie and me in a similar place in our lives in a few years. After we completed our dissertations and established ourselves as researchers in our fields. But I was proud of Amira and Bilial. As people, as professionals and as our friends.

JAMIE

After our time with Amira and Bilial, we drove on to San Francisco to visit Blair. She was living in the city and was a practicing attorney with a good environmental law firm. We hadn't seen her or been to San Francisco for a long time. She had a cute one-bedroom apartment with a beautiful view of the bay. She insisted we stay with her. Fortunately, her living room sofa bed was comfortable.

BLAIR (friend)

It had been quite some time since I'd seen Robin and Jamie. Studying for their comprehensives had occupied all their time. It was great to get together again. We, including my boyfriend, Sam, celebrated the completion of their doctoral courses with dim sum at Hang Ah restaurant in Chinatown. It was funny they had both eaten there before they knew each other. What an amazing coincidence.

I love it when my friends are happy and when everything is going well for them. But I did detect an undercurrent of anxiety now that they were closing in on their goal. I understood that feeling. Ready to play but will you be picked for a team? I was fortunate to find a good positon with a great law firm. They were faced with having to find two good jobs. And in close proximity.

🌿 🌿 🌿

ROBIN

After our trip visiting old friends, it was back to Davis to write our dissertations. That was another year of hard work. Then I had to defend my dissertation with the entomology faculty committee. I based my work on how a beehive naturally protects itself from parasites. Which is for sick honeybees to voluntarily leave a hive or even be forcibly expelled by hive mates. But if a parasite infestation becomes too great for the beehive to deal with, the result is colony collapse. None of this is new information. What was new in my dissertation was the comparison I made with the human body. How an outside incursion can lead to an immune reaction that—if the human immune system cannot cope—may result in "body collapse."

Furthermore, I hypothesized a method based on how infected cells could be treated in the human system without overloading the immune system and causing an autoimmune reaction. I based this theory on how we treat hives when they are overloaded with parasites. The trick would be to identify the immune system "triggers." This had potential applications for people and for honeybees. My interdisciplinary Ph.D. in entomology and biology was awarded. Yay!

JAMIE

My dissertation was on the microbial plants needed to maintain health. Soil microbes can activate a plant's own defenses and even have a vaccination-like effect. Identifying and encouraging their growth—rather than the eradication of these valuable organisms—has direct parallels with what we have learned about the microorganisms that live in humans.

Plants also communicate with each other when they are invaded by a pathogen. This transmission takes place through the soil. Through the roots of one plant to the roots of other plants. This allows neighboring plants and trees to activate their defense systems. I theorized that finding the beneficial microbes would help our understanding of how to keep plants healthy as well as how our own immune systems can be stimulated. And it was likely these microbes would also be found in the plants themselves just as they are found in us. Therefore, there could be plants that would have the effect of triggering our immune response. The committee of the botany faculty awarded my interdisciplinary Ph.D. Sheng! Translation is "Victory!"

🌿 🌿 🌿

ROBIN

Our relationship was so important. So helpful to us in accomplishing our goals. Both of us achieving doctoral degrees. We encouraged each other and studied together. When either of us felt overwhelmed, we shared a laugh or a gripe. We appreciated and understood the effort it took. It made a big difference and brought us even closer.

Jamie was great. However, he did have an annoying trait of giving me directions about how to do everyday tasks. When he did that in China, it was understandable since I was unfamiliar with the customs. But in the U.S., it seemed overbearing. For example, when I was driving he would say, "That car is tailgating you. Move into another lane." Or he would tell me to watch out for a curb or an uneven sidewalk. Or to be careful with a kitchen knife because I was holding it wrong. I know he was coming from a good place. That he was looking out for me. But it felt bossy and overprotective. I was becoming irritated and snappy. I decided to do what my parents did when they had an issue with each other. Communicate. I told him I needed him to trust that I could handle the common tasks of my life without his guidance. Oh dear. He looked wounded. But he said he understood and he dialed it back. Most of the time.

JAMIE

Robin was wonderful. She was perfect. Almost perfect. She was a little messy. Piles of magazines, articles and books everywhere. A disorganized desk buried under stacks of projects. And clothes stuffed in drawers. Things like that. But she put up with my always misplacing things. I could never find my keys or my shoes or my mug or sunglasses. Sometimes even my toothbrush.

She did sometimes rush into things without thinking them through. A gung-ho overconfidence. Maybe it was caused by some lingering hyperactivity. I tried to slow her down. Get her to think not only about her actions but about the results of those actions.

And Robin recognized the inequality of opportunity that existed. That people of means got further in life. She knew her parents had given her advantages others didn't have. She wanted to prove herself. That she could do everything and could do it by herself.

ROBIN

It was a big adjustment being with someone else. I was used to doing everything on my own. I was independent. Jamie was too. But I think we worked it out. Thank goodness we loved each other so much.

🌿 🌿 🌿

JAMIE

When you get a stipend, a university can have a proprietary interest in your dissertation. We were lucky. With help from our faculty advisor, Sylvia, we negotiated keeping ownership while UC Davis kept publishing rights. The ownership was important to us because our dissertations could help open doors for us. Applying for grants, fellowships, jobs.

ROBIN

Our dream was to get research fellowships for field research in Manu National Park in Peru. We wanted to find new medicinal plants and varied insect colonies. Why Manu in Peru? We studied a lot of possible locations. The Brazilian Amazon, Panama, Papua New Guinea. Any of them would have been great. And our hope was that someday we would go to all of them. And other places too. But our first choice was Manu. It was an amazing place. The greatest biodiversity in the world with the largest possibility of undiscovered plant and insect species. And 80 percent of the park was a core zone available only for scientific research. We felt certain we would find what we were looking for in Manu National Park.

JAMIE

We investigated grants and fellowships. There were opportunities. But not for both of us in the same geographic location. And we couldn't find any for field research. We were confident we could get jobs. Go the same route as Bilial and Amira. But we would have to compromise on the type of research we did. We considered taking out loans to pay for our field research. But where would we do our lab work afterward? While we tried to figure out our next step, we resigned ourselves to continuing our lab assistant jobs.

ROBIN

Everyone was going in different directions. During the past year, Annie had moved in with Jake. Now they were moving to the Wine Country where she could work for a wine consortium while he got his cybersecurity business up and running.

Frannie did get a job at Google. But no one helped her. It was on her own merit. Everyone was moving on. Jamie and I felt stuck and frustrated. Then Blair called me.

BLAIR (friend)
One of my firm's clients, Dr. Casey Dee Roy, was a wealthy environmentalist. Like billionaire wealthy. He had sold his internet company Xgenesis for $5 billion. Now he was financing ecological and health research. I told him about Robin and Jamie. He asked me to have them send their resumes and dissertations to him.

JAMIE
We immediately sent them electronically. A week later, we got a call from Dr. Roy. He invited us to meet with him at the Mountain View headquarters of his new corporation —TransFormancy.

Before our meeting we researched his company. The building was impressive. Three stories. Modern. Lots of glass. But what really excited us was the description of what the company did. Biomedical, agricultural, ecological research. All with the goal of improving the health of people and the environment. Could this be the opportunity we were looking for? We were excited. And nervous.

Mountain View, California

ROBIN
I remember my surprise when we first saw Casey Dee Roy. He was an average height. Maybe five foot, nine. But he

was striking looking. Though I thought he had the face and complexion of an Indian warrior, I couldn't place what kind of Indian he resembled. Native American? South American? Indian from India? And I didn't recognize the ethnicity of his name. I did detect a slight British accent. He had a warm smile, light brown hair and translucent blue eyes. He was possibly in his late 50s. But something about him felt much older. It was easy to believe that Dr. Roy was smart enough to make a fortune.

Casey Dee, as Dr. Roy wanted to be called, made us feel welcome and relaxed. Rather than face him across his desk we all sat in comfortable chairs around a coffee table. He wanted to know everything about us. Starting with our childhoods and families. It felt as if we were talking to an old friend. I told him how my ADHD led to my interest in insects, my mom's illness, my desire to find a cure for MS, my closeness with my family. Jamie talked about his early years involved in farming, his love for trees and plants, his father's death, his relationship with his mother. We did not mention our special abilities.

Casey Dee wanted to know how we met. He laughed at our error-prone meetings. He was a good listener and I felt his genuine interest in us. Then he asked us what we wanted to do. We told him our dream was to find undiscovered plants and insects that could lead to cures for cancer and MS.

JAMIE

Casey Dee thanked us for sharing our lives with him. He said it was only fair he tell us about himself. He was part British and part Indian, from India. He had been divorced for a long time and had a grown daughter. He was originally a medical researcher but part of him wanted to make money. So he had spent the past 20 years in the pursuit of wealth. Now the other part of him was following his passion to improve people's lives and protect the environment. His financial success allowed him to start TransFormancy, the enterprise to achieve that purpose.

He explained, "I believe they are identical goals. The better that people's lives are, the less likely they are to destroy the natural world. For instance, when health and income improve, families have fewer children. Fewer people mean less pressure on the environment."

ROBIN

Then he said he wanted to hire us. And if we accepted, he would fund our field research. He added, "When you return, you'll work here in TransFormancy's labs. You will try to turn your collected specimens into treatments for MS and cancer. Have you thought of where you want to go?"

Jamie answered, "Manu National Park in Peru."

Casey Dee looked uncomfortable. And he was silent for several minutes. Finally he said, "I guess I am surprised because I went to Manu a long time ago. Why do you want to go there instead of the Brazilian Amazon or the Panamanian jungle or anywhere else?"

Jamie and I took turns enthusiastically explaining why Manu was where we wanted to go.

Casey Dee responded, "I just want you to be sure. Manu is fascinating but when I was there it was a dangerous place with a lot of unknowns. I doubt it has changed in that regard. But perhaps you may learn as much about yourselves as you do about the plants and insects. Things you never imagined."

I said, "We think we know what the challenges are in a remote rainforest and we are confident we can handle them."

Casey Dee sighed and asked, "Do you believe in fate?"

JAMIE
Casey Dee's assistant, Andy, took us on a tour of TransFormancy. He said the staff called it TF or TransForm. It was exciting to see how well-equipped the labs were. Everyone was friendly. It seemed like a pleasant place. Even a cheerful place. Andy told us the research staff was given a free hand to work on projects they believed in. They were happy to be there.

Before we left, Andy gave us his direct line. As our liaison, he would help plan our trip. Making all the arrangements. Flights, hotels as needed, ground transportation, permits, guides.

DR. CASEY DEE ROY (CEO)
From their dissertations, I could tell they were both able to think outside the box. I liked that. And after spending time getting to know them, I was even more impressed. They

shared a dedication to their goals of finding cures for cancer and MS. And they were committed to the ecological health of the planet. They were a bright young couple. Well matched.

I hoped that Jamie and Robin would find what they were looking for in Manu National Park. And become a real asset to TransFormancy. I felt they would fit in well here. But more than anything, I wanted them to return safely. However, I did have a sense there was something they weren't telling me. But no one—including me—reveals everything. Not immediately.

JAMIE

Robin was excited. On the drive back to Davis, she was talking about all the planning and preparation we had to do. About Casey Dee. About TransFormancy. I was quiet. Finally, she asked if something was wrong. I said that it was perfect. Too perfect. Too easy. "It hasn't been easy," she said. "We have worked hard for a long time to prepare ourselves for this opportunity." She was right about that. I felt better. But why did Casey Dee ask us about fate? Don't we make our own destiny?

🌿   🌿   🌿

ROBIN

It takes a lot of work and preparation to ensure a successful field research trip. We had met with Casey Dee in October so we completed our university research assistant fall quarter commitment. After visits to our families, we finally gave up our Viridian apartment and relocated to Mountain View, the heart of Silicon Valley. Our new apartment had two bedrooms. That was good for when we had family and friends visit. It was a lot more expensive but we were earning good salaries working for TransFormancy.

We saw Amira and Bilial as often as working, sleep-deprived parents of a baby girl could manage. And we were busy setting up our labs. Jamie's was on the second floor. Mine was on the third floor.

JAMIE

We worked closely with Andy on the planning for the trip. The most difficult part of the process was getting an entry permit from the Peruvian government for the Manu core area. Eventually everything was in place for a late May departure. The timing was good. Although rain was always possible, the official rainy season would be over.

Peru

ROBIN

The flight to Cusco, Peru, with a stop in Panama City, was eight hours. We spent a couple of days seeing the sights in Cusco. A lovely city. The original Inca capital and later a Spanish colony. Then we took a 12-hour bus ride to Atalaya, a town at the entrance to the park. I had never experienced a more breathtaking bus ride. Literally. Twists and turns. Sometimes looking several hundred feet straight down a mountainside into a densely foliage-covered ravine. Several times the passengers had to get off the bus while the driver placed boards down to drive over washed away sections of the road. And I can testify that it was possible to sleep sitting up while the bus bumped along.

Then eight hours by boat—a covered motor launch—to Boca Manu. And another eight hours on the river to the park. I didn't know a river could be so winding. So scenic. So slow. We saw countless bird species, capybaras, giant river otters, caimans and even river dolphins. It gave us an opportunity to appreciate the country, the people. And to experience the sometimes misty, rainy and windy climate. The boat had no side canvases to roll down. We were exposed to rain and crosswinds. Along the way, I practiced my Spanish with some of the other passengers. I was improving. Jamie was picking up words and phrases.

While we found traveling by bus and boat to be an interesting experience, we decided we didn't want this slow and occasionally uncomfortable trip back. On our return, we would take the faster route. Flying form Boca Manu to Cusco.

JAMIE

Our private guide met us in Boca Manu and continued with us. His name was Manuel Mendez Montero. We called him ThreeM. We liked him right away. He had a brawny build and a personality to match. About four or five inches shorter than me. Black hair. Big black mustache. And a passable command of English.

ROBIN

ThreeM had supplies we would need. Tents, food, water. And something we didn't need. Bug repellent. He also had a rifle. He said it was necessary for protection against wild animals living in the jungle. But only he, as an authorized guide, was permitted to have one.

THREE~M (guide)

I see we get along good. Señor Jamie and Señora Robin were good people. I love Manu. I love forest. Animals. Trees. Everything. I much learn from scientists I guide. They learn much from me. I tell about people that live in forest long, long time. Hundreds of people. Many different tribes. Many tribes make no contact. Most called Mashco-Piro. They move around much. They hunt. Use bow and arrow. Guns kill many animals. No good for jungle. They fish. They grow crops. Yucca, cotton. Outside people must stay far from tribes. Colds, flu, diseases from outside people can kill tribe. Wipe them out.

Park feels danger. Men want logging, gas, mining from park. Talk of government building roads from Cusco to park scares me. Make logging, gas, mining more easy.

JAMIE

ThreeM had his own covered launch. But the last eight hours of our final leg on the brown Manu River seemed endless. At least the weather was better. No more rain and wind. We were impatient to get to our destination. We learned a lot about the park from ThreeM. The people, animals, plants. We ate onboard but stopped occasionally to stretch our legs and use nature's restroom. ThreeM cooked a pretty good arroz con bagre. Rice with freshly caught catfish. Finally we arrived at our destination, Cocha Cashu Biological Station. CCBS for short.

Manu National Park, Peru

ROBIN

The core area was immense: 3,787,000 acres out of the park's total 4,448,000 acres. Cocha Cashu was located inside this strict protection zone in the middle of the Manu watershed. It was basic. The research station was comprised of an office, a bathhouse and a kitchen. The researchers camped beside the trails by the station. The intermittent internet connection was mostly down.

We packed lightly. Jamie and I could, and did occasionally, wear each other's clothes. We each brought two pair of unisex, convertible quick-dry cargo pants and two quick-dry shirts. Biodegradable detergent. Hats, of course. Lightweight waterproof hiking boots, quick-drying socks. Sunblock. Most of our gear was for our research. Hundreds of mostly small plastic tubes for our sample collections. Also preservatives and swabbing supplies. Scientists and researchers are allowed to collect samples but cannot affect the natural system. ThreeM introduced us to two local men, Elias and Ruben, from the more integrated Matsigenka Tribe. They would help carry our supplies on our excursions deeper into the park.

JAMIE

At daybreak we were awakened by the incredible calls of hundreds of birds. A comparatively small assortment of the more than 1,000 bird species living in the rainforest. At first we kept our exploration close to the station. It was hot and humid. It didn't have to be raining for my skin to feel wet. Robin fared better since she had already experienced a tropical forest in Costa Rica. But it exhausted me. It took me at least five or six days to adjust to the conditions.

The second week we went farther into the rainforest. The green lushness was amazing. The canopy of majestic trees shaded the forest floor. It was a decomposing ecosphere dominated by microorganisms feeding off decaying leaves. Fungi and lichens were everywhere. The thousands of tree species were often interwoven with vines. All kinds of vines—thick and thin, curved and straight—hung like ropes. Except for the occasional patch of sunlight through the canopy, we couldn't tell if the sky was cloudy or sunny. Where light did penetrate to the ground, there was an explosion of plant life. Each trying to gain a foothold and dominate the ray of sunshine. It was an overwhelmingly proliferate and extravagant scene.

ROBIN

The rainforest was not calm and peaceful. It was a riot of sounds. Birds, frogs, cicadas, monkeys and occasional buzzing insects. The noisy howling of red howler monkeys. The "wah, wah, wah" calls of capuchins. The squeaks and chirps of tamarins. The screeches and barks of spider monkeys. Nor was the terrain always flat. Sometimes we scrambled on upslopes and skidded on downslopes. And sometimes—after torrents of rain—everything was slippery.

JAMIE

I was searching for rare plants I thought had a good chance of being undetected or untested. When I found such plants, I took a sample of their leaves and collected either their spores, bulbs, seeds or pods. I also gathered fungi and soil samples. Sometimes the trees helped by telling me about healthy symbiotic relationships they had with specific plants and fungi. Even though the park was established in 1973 and hundreds of scientists have studied every aspect of the forest, it was amazingly rich in biodiversity— 20,000 plant species—that there were still new discoveries to be made.

ROBIN

The number of different bees, over 650 species, was an example of the variety of colony insect life in Manu. It meant a lot of work. I took notes and video recorded my observations of their hives as well ant nests. I looked for the chemical communicators—touch and smell—that affected insects. I took swabs of their pheromones and chemical trails. I gathered samples of microbes, including bacteria and mites, found in colonies. I also collected dead and dying insects. They could tell me a great deal about what went wrong within a hive or colony. And I swabbed for allomones, chemical substances that a species releases to protect itself. An example of an allomone is what plants produce to protect themselves against insect attacks. In this regard, my research and Jamie's overlapped.

THREE~M (guide)

Two weeks more they want go more in forest. Along Providencia River. It runs into Manu River. I not happy. Much away from Cocha Cashu. Much danger. Loggers float trees down rivers out of Manu. Loggers have guns. But Señor Jamie and Señora Robin want to go. I no want to scare them. I tell

them, "If I see danger and say, 'Move behind me.' Do that. If I say, 'Run.' Do that. Do what I say." They say, "Yes." I talk to Elias and Ruben in Yine, their language. They say, "OK." Me they trust.

We ride my boat up Providencia. When Señor and Señora want, we stop. Put up tents. Walk. Look. I go first. We walk by river. Ears open. Listen for sound of buzz saws. Three days. I see nothing bad. I see jaguar on other side of river.

JAMIE

The Providencia, a tributary of the Manu River, was as rich in plants and insects as we could have wished. It was amazing how the varieties differed from one area to another. We camped along the way and then studied the area surrounding our campsite. On the fourth day we moved further up the river.

As we hiked along, I heard a tree in the distance ahead of us. It was screaming. All the trees were upset. I could feel their anxiety vibrating through my feet. Then the screaming tree fell silent. All the trees became quiet. Now I only felt their fear. I wanted to tell ThreeM. But how could I explain this experience—this phenomenon—to him. And since I wasn't sure what it meant, I didn't want to alarm Robin.

ROBIN

We were deeper into the rainforest than we had ever been. The heat was stifling. The forest floor was often muddy and slippery. It was difficult to stay on our feet. My instinct was to reach for vines and tree trunks but that was risky. In shades of gray and black gloom—I didn't always know what I was grasping. Was it a vine or snake hanging from a tree?

Sweat was pouring off all of us. The darkness was oppressive. And when a rare ray of light did penetrate to the forest floor, the glare was blinding. The constant shrieking of birds added to my anxiety. I had to remind myself why we were here. We were searching for healing discoveries. But why here? What were we thinking? This area was dangerous. Full of natural risks. It felt as if the forest was our enemy. But I was wrong. The real enemy walked on two legs.

THREE~M (guide)

We make turn. Where land and river bend. I see 12 men—maybe more—in open space they make with big cut down mahogany tree. They sit. Cooking, eating. I see rifles by trees trunks. I stop. I talk soft, "Back up. Go back." We move back. But one man see us. He yells. He grabs gun. I yell, "Run!" Señor, Señora run. I hear gun shot. I turn. Face men. They run to us with guns. I shoot at them. Want to scare men away.

ROBIN

The sound of a gunshot was terrifying. We knew immediately we were in danger. Elias and Ruben were behind us and when we turned to run, they were in front of us. Then, as if they never existed, they melted into the forest. As I took a quick look back, I saw ThreeM go down. Jamie also saw him get shot. He grabbed for my hand but we couldn't run holding hands. I followed him as we ran as fast as we had ever run in our lives. ThreeM had made us aware of the natural dangers of the forest. Of snakes, spiders, jaguars. He taught us to move cautiously and keep our eyes open. None of that mattered now. We were only aware of great danger. Of men chasing us. Intent on killing us.

JAMIE

I heard the trees. They yelled at me. "Run this way. Run that way." Our original path along the river was impossible to follow. It was gone. We were running through the forest. Following the trees' instructions. We heard the men behind us. When they saw us, they fired. We could hear their bullets embed in tree trunks. We were tripping over roots and dead branches. Tearing through vines and spider webs. We barely managed to keep our feet under us as we slid in mud. We jumped and climbed over fallen tree trunks. Vines pulled at us. Needles and thorns tore at our clothes and skin. The men were still in pursuit. They could hear us running. They were excited. This was a hunt for them. There were so many men chasing us. We couldn't seem to lose them. One tree yelled, "Duck!" I pulled Robin down just before a bullet flew over our heads. Another tree shouted to get behind it. Then we heard a bullet hit the tree's trunk.

I felt more fear of being captured than of being shot. What would they do to us? What would they do to Robin? I was leading Robin as the trees directed me. The heat and humidity were taking a toll. We were growing tired but our fear kept us going. I could hear them behind us. The men were fanning out. Surrounding us.

Then a tree yelled, "Jamie! Stop! Climb me!" It was the shock of hearing my name that made me stop. I started to push Robin up the tree. A huge tree with large buttressed, undulating roots that spread out in all directions. These roots had hollows and grooves that made climbing easier. The last major root reached as high as the first massive limb. At least 50 feet up. From there we climbed from one giant limb to another as they spread out in all directions in an inverted pyramid form. We supported our climb by grabbing vines that hung down. With the last of our strength we reached the thickest part of the tree's canopy, ranging out into a crown.

We could hear some of the men below us. We couldn't see the ground. We hoped they couldn't see us.

ROBIN

I knew that Jamie was being directed by the trees. I didn't hesitate when he began pushing me to climb one. As we ascended the roots, bats flew out of hollows and startled me. I almost lost my grip but Jamie steadied me.

The tree was immense. Gigantic. When we reached its canopy, we were over 100 feet from the ground. And we were only halfway to the top. We were winded but we didn't dare breathe heavy. We could hear the men calling to each other around us. Below us. I understood their Spanish. Telling each other to look this way. Look that way. After a half hour of not being able to hear or see us, they said, "Let's go back. They will die anyway. They will never find their way out."

We waited a long time. We wanted to be sure they were gone. The light was fading. Darkness came. We didn't know where we were. And we weren't going to start looking in the dark. We stayed in the tree. We clung to each other tightly so we wouldn't fall off the crook of the tree limb we straddled. There were a lot of insects in the tree but I kept them—especially the biting ones—away from us. I sort of dozed off and on during the night but I heard Jamie talking to the tree. Thanking the tree for saving us. Thanking all the trees for helping us.

JAMIE

With dawn's light I realized we were in a ceiba tree. A rain-forest colossus often growing more than 200 feet high. And with a massive width. The Maya considered it the Tree of Life. It certainly was a tree of life for us. We climbed down. We didn't know where we were. We didn't have anything. Our backpacks were gone. Thrown away while we were running. But I wasn't worried. I assured Robin the trees would help us find our way back to Cocha Cashu. Then we would alert the authorities and form a search party. Hopefully we would find ThreeM alive.

I asked the trees to lead us. And they did. "Come this way." "Go that way." We walked and walked. We were thirsty and hungry. We saw puddles of water but we feared they were contaminated with parasites. Robin said she wished she had watched more jungle survivor shows. I couldn't have agreed more. At last we came to a clearing.

ROBIN

Seven huts were arranged in a semicircle. They looked like beach shade tents or cabanas. Open in the front and only about five feet high. But instead of nylon they were made with palm fronds. The little camp looked and felt abandoned. Since nomadic indigenous people often move, the deserted site was not unusual.

Then I saw an old person sitting in front of one of the huts. How had I not seen her before? The light? My wooziness from hunger and thirst? She was stirring a small pot over a little fire. We approached and I spoke to her in Spanish but she didn't understand. Too bad I didn't know the Yine language. We gestured that we were thirsty and hungry. She gave us a toothless smile and waved us to sit down. Dipping her ladle into the soup, she offered it to us. We gratefully slurped the broth. It wasn't just good. It was great. In the way that food tastes great when you are extremely hungry. She offered us more. Passing the ladle between us, we drank more. We looked up to her to thank her. She was gone! How could she disappear without our noticing?

I asked. "Where did she go?"

Jamie answered, "What do you mean 'she'? The old person was a 'he.'"

I responded, "She or he. It doesn't matter. It's weird. Vanishing like that. But the pot is still here. Let's finish the soup. We'll need all our strength to get out of the forest."

JAMIE
When we stood up I suddenly felt unsteady. Did I get up too fast? I looked at Robin. She was trembling. We both began to shake, to stagger. What was happening? Was it food poisoning? Would food poisoning take effect that fast? Or were we purposely poisoned? Was that why the old one disappeared? Our fear was intense. We hugged each other

tightly. If we were going to die, we would go embracing each other. The world was spinning around us. We had a powerful sensation of falling—up!

And then ... and then ... and then ... it happened.

No more Jamie and Robin. No more male or female. We were something different. A new kind of being. One being with two minds—a dual consciousness.

8

THE MEANING OF US

Somewhere Along the Providencia River

CHENDELL

We were transformed. Into what? Into CHENDELL. We were two halves of one person. We had the thoughts of each of us. And yet we were unified. We felt like "we." We felt like one person. What did we look like? Streamlined. Eurasian. One green-colored eye and one dark brown-colored eye. Our shoulder-length hair was streaked black and auburn.

We recognized how different we were. Our senses were extremely acute. Our strength was exceptionally strong. Our brain cells had exploded in number, making our mind light-ning-quick and smart. And though we didn't realize it at the time, our powers had increased. Not just with trees, plants and insects but also with other living creatures. All of nature would be our ally. But we didn't have time to dwell on what had happened to us or why. We could hear trees screaming from many miles away. We could even hear the bugs and the birds shrieking. We had to act. Our purpose was clear. We began running in the direction of the cries for help.

This time our run through the forest was easier. We just forced aside the vines and branches. Jumped over tumbled tree trunks and small streams. The trees kept yelling, "Hurry! Hurry!" Then we came to the river. It was wide. We saw black caiman in the river. They looked hungry. With our greatly increased strength, we dragged a large thick fallen tree trunk to the shore and pushed it into the water. With our feet, we flattened two dense, sizeable branches to use as paddles. We shoved off and straddled the log.

Two caimans swam toward us. Larger than their North American alligator cousins. And deadly. We hit the first one—the smaller of the two—on the snout with our heavy branches. It moved off. The second one was much bigger and more aggressive. Possibly a male. He first went for our nearest leg. We quickly raised it high enough to avoid his bite. We whacked him with our branches as he swam under our log. He circled back and upended it, sending us into the water. That's when we remembered something we read about the eyes of an alligator being the most vulnerable. We called in the cavalry. Bees. The caiman was about to bite us and pull us under when we jammed our branches into his cavernous tooth-lined mouth. He crushed the branches like toothpicks. We were next. But just in time—the bees arrived. They stung the caiman's eyes. He immediately backed off and dived. We knew he wasn't coming back. He'd had enough of our company.

In the slow-moving water, our tree trunk had caught on a snag in the river. We swam fast enough to reach it and climbed on before it broke loose. By lying prone on the log and using our hands to paddle, we reached the opposite shore.

We began running again. But we only got about a hundred yards when, in our rush, we stepped on the tail of an Amazon coral snake. We knew we were in trouble. The snake's instinctive reaction was to strike at us. We turned just as it launched its attack. Our reflexive reaction was to jump back but it bit our leg. We felt nothing. The snake's fangs had only torn our pants. Our skin had become covered with a thick bark. With its fangs embedded, we shook our leg hard—throwing off the bark and the snake with it.

We ran on. But the screams of distant trees drowned out the warning of the tree we just passed. A 300-pound jaguar, nestled in its branches, sprung at us with a predator's silence. To the jaguar, we were running prey. And he didn't know we were there to help the forest. He hit us from behind. Knocking us to the ground. Fortunately our upright posture prevented him from sinking his teeth into our head. Just as a jaguar uses his powerful bite to crush the skull of a caiman, our skull could have been punctured. We rolled around to face him as he lunged at our face. We held off his attack by grabbing his neck. Our boosted strength allowed us to keep his snarling, gaping jaws from biting us. Then with a quick move, we used our free hand to punch him as hard as we could on the nose. It was a tough, painful blow. His nose was bloodied. Startled and confused, he moved back. His usual prey—deer, snakes, sloths, tapirs—don't punch. We took advantage of his pause to leap to our feet. We had no desire to seriously hurt him. We waved our arms and shouted as loud as we could. Our wild display made us seem bigger and more threatening. We could see him thinking this wasn't worth it. He moved off.

No time to contemplate or even look for more dangers. We continued our run along the river until we saw the movement of men. We stopped and surveyed the scene. They were the dozen or more illegal loggers who had chased us a day ago. The same greedy, treacherous men. But we were not the same.

They were working on the trunk of a mahogany tree. This time they had posted two armed men to watch for intruders. Then we spotted ThreeM. He was alive but in bad shape. He had a crude bloody bandage around one arm. His hands were tied together. They had beaten him. We could hear them taunting him with threats. Once they cut down the tree and dragged it to the river, they were going to tie him to its trunk. And as they floated it down the river, they would roll it. Watching him slowly drown. Their version of waterboarding. We had to act fast. We had to stop ThreeM—and the tree— from dying. Mahogany wood is extremely dense but soon the cut would be too deep for the tree to recover.

We called on all the bees in the area. The insects swarmed the three men who were wielding saws. They screamed and tried to bat the bees away. The other men yelled at them to run to the river. To jump into the water. The men tried to run away but the bees followed them. Clinging to them. Stinging them over and over. One man fell as he lost consciousness. The other two were semiconscious as they writhed in pain on the ground. Their exposed skin was covered in swollen, red bumps. Not a pleasant sight.

Then we guided several tarantula-hawk wasps to attack two other men. The effect of this solitary wasp's sting is short-lived but so violently electric that almost no one can continue to walk and talk. The men dropped to the ground screaming and thrashing in severe agony. One managed to get up but his anguish caused him to run headlong into a tree. He was knocked out cold. The other man, in a disoriented state, tried to crawl to the river. Instead he went deeper into the forest. After a few minutes he screamed again, "Snake! Help me!" Then silence. A snakebite had paralyzed him. Maybe killed him. If it was the coral snake that tried to bite us, it was still angry.

We directed a giant centipede—12 inches long—to skitter inside the boot of another logger and bite him. Shock and disbelief crossed his face as the excruciating pain radiated up from his foot. He shouted for help and three of the men rushed to his aid. That's when bullet ants attacked them. Hundreds and hundreds of these ants teemed over them. Climbing under their pant legs and biting them. The agony caused by these inch-long ants is comparable to a gunshot. With shattering screams, they ripped their pants off and tried to dislodge the ants with their hands. Now their hands were being bitten. The effect was a temporary paralysis to their legs and hands. They couldn't move or defend themselves. They lay on the ground screeching in agony. At the mercy of the ants.

The remaining men were terrified and confused. They looked everywhere—to the ground, to the sky—to try to protect themselves. They didn't know what they had to defend against. They yelled to each other, "What's going on? Do you see anything?"

One of them was looking up when he should have been looking down. We called upon a Brazilian wandering spider. An extremely venomous spider that doesn't make a web. It walks the forest floor searching for prey. It found the man's ankle. He grabbed his ankle and fell as he shrieked in pain. And then the man went into spasms, gasping for air. He could not overcome the poison surging through his body.

Though we were standing at the edge of the clearing, we had been undetected. Our body was magically camouflaged with bark and our hair was made of leaves. We threw off our facade and stepped forward as CHENDELL. Someone the men never expected to see in the forest. They looked at us in disbelief. A tall Eurasian with black and auburn hair. One dark-colored eye, one green-colored eye. Their surprise turned to anger as they realized we must have had something to do with everything that happened. They grabbed their rifles and fired at us. The bullets slammed into our chest but still we stood. The bullets were embedded in the thick bark that covered our torso.

They had had enough. "Dios ayudame a vivir"—God help me live—they wailed as they ran toward the river. They didn't get far. We asked an ipê tree to drop a large branch. It hit one of the men. Knocking him out. Then we directed vines from another tree to entangle the other man. As he struggled he became more ensnared and was strangled unconscious.

We rushed to ThreeM. Untied him and gave him the loggers' water. We were helping him to his feet when the trees yelled, "Watch out!" We suddenly found ourselves surrounded by six men who had recovered enough to try to stop us. We were standing under the tornillo tree where ThreeM had been bound. At our request the tree dropped a straight five-foot branch into our hands. A fighting handstick for us to use.

We let ThreeM sink back to the ground and stepped away from him. The encircling men shifted with us. We rotated in place. Waiting for them to make the first move. Alert to their expressions and their slightest movements. When they charged we used our kung fu training. First striking one man in front of us with one end of the branch and then immediately thrusting the other end into a man behind us. We swung our weapon around. Hitting one man while keeping the others off guard and at a distance. When they came at us again, we flipped over their heads so we were behind them. We threw one of the men over our shoulder and blocked another man's attack with our left arm. With a quick, powerful right fist, we knocked him unconscious. We instantly turned to send a kick into the body of the flipped man as he was getting to his feet. That sent him flying into an acai palm tree. We slammed his head against the tree trunk and he went down. Three men left. We assumed The Horse stance. Feet apart, a squat position leaning slightly backward with a low center of gravity. We pulled our fists alongside our hips. As the men attacked we employed a lightning-speed chop to one man's throat. And then used a zigzag motion kick into the other man's groin. We spun again to land another kick into the third man's chest.

One guy got up and started running to the river. We ran after him and tackled him. We caught his legs and pulled him down. He turned over to fight us. We wrestled with him and traded punches. He was strong. We were stronger. His fist hit our shoulder hard. The one that had been fractured in Sequoia. We winced but came back with a good blow to his jaw. He was knocked out. We tied him with a vine. We went back to the clearing where we found some rope and tied up the other men. All was quiet except for an occasional groan or pain-filled cry.

ThreeM was still slumped against a tree. Awake but weak. He didn't know who we were. He didn't care. He was just thankful to be saved. We helped him get up. He could barely walk. We half-carried him to the river. There we found the loggers' two boats. After putting him in one of the launches, we poured sandy dirt into the outboard motor of the other boat. We went back to collect as many of the weapons, saws and axes as possible—and threw them into the river. The trunk of the mahogany tree they had cut down the day before was secured to the shore. We untied it and watched as it floated downstream. What a waste of a beautiful living tree.

We pushed off and started down the river. But the surrounding trees were alarmed. They warned us. Someone on the shore was taking aim at us. Had he recovered or had he hidden from us?

We threw our body over ThreeM. A bullet grazed our back. Bark had again formed to provide protective armor. Then two bullets bounced off the outboard motor. We realized he was trying to disable it. That was an alarming possibility. We were faced with the choice of using our body to protect ThreeM or the motor. But before we had to make a decision, five scarlet macaws flew down and attacked him. These beautiful, large and highly intelligent birds had been feasting on the plentiful bacaba berries of a bacaba palm tree by the river. With their extremely powerful beaks, they tore at his head and face. The man tried to hold them off by swinging his rifle. One of the birds, using its strong flexible toes, caught it on a swing and dropped it in the river. With the screeching birds in pursuit, the man ran into the forest.

We were certainly surprised and elated by what had happened. We didn't know birds would come to our aid. Then we remembered that years ago a crow, at a tree's demand, returned a stolen pastry. With that memory came the realization that trees and birds have a symbiotic relationship. The macaws enjoyed the tree's berries and the tree told them to help us. At that time, we still didn't realize we could directly connect with birds and other animals.

🍃   🍃   🍃

After we had traveled two hours on the Providencia River, we tied up and examined ThreeM's arm. The bullet had gone through his bicep without hitting the bone but the wound looked infected. We found a tawari tree. And with the tree's permission, we took some of its bark. We put the bark on his wound and secured it with a vine. This would help fight the infection. We also brewed some of the bark in a tea for him. With food we found on the boat, he was able to regain some strength. We located ThreeM's launch tied up downstream and spent the night along the bank. In the morning, ThreeM was doing better mentally and physically. He said, "You look much like Señor Jamie and much like Señora Robin. But you are one. What make you one? Magic?" We told him, "Yes, it was magic. And now we must go back to where it happened to try to undo it." Then ThreeM asked us if we were a man or a woman. We were startled by his question. It was what we had wondered about the old one, the shaman. We had not considered that the same speculation would apply to us. It was all the same. People needed to put everyone in a category.

In our khaki pants and shirt, we looked as we always did. We felt as Robin always did. We felt as Jamie always did. Did our dual minds see and feel what each of us wanted to see and feel? How did we want to perceive ourselves? Did it matter? These were questions for another time or for others to worry about. Now we had to find the shaman.

We asked, "Can you take the boat back to Cocha Cashu by yourself?" He said he could make it to a Matsigenka village where the Providencia and Manu rivers meet. They would help him the rest of the way. We were confident he knew his forest and its people. We divided up the food and water and saw him off.

We took our boat up the river again. Always staying close to the bank on the opposite side of our run-in with the loggers. We were confident that we could handle another fight with them. But we had another purpose on our mind now. We had to find the old person—the shaman. We had to undo what had made us one person.

The trees helped us determine where to bank our boat. The best spot closest to the deserted native encampment. Once on foot, they guided us to our destination. The seven small huts. We feared that we would not be able to find the shaman. But there was the same person. Sitting in the same spot and stirring the same pot. Then we got a surprise. The old one looked up and greeted us in Spanish, "Buenas dias, CHENDELL."

We approached and sat down. Conversing in Spanish, we said, "You know our name. What is your name?"

The shaman replied, "Birú."

We asked, "Why did you make us one person?"

Birú answered, "You found me. Those who find me are looking for something. You found it. You were meant to be one person. You will protect what cannot protect itself. It is your fate. Your purpose."

In our deepest core these words rang true. But we had another question. "Can we be two separate people again?"

"You can be Robin and you can be Jamie. Stroke both sides of your hair two times while you keep your brown eye open, then two times while you keep your green eye open. Feel yourselves pulling apart. You will be 'she' and 'he' again."

"And if we are to continue the fight to save our natural world, can we be CHENDELL again?"

"Hold each other. You both close your eyes and stroke the

other's hair three times. Feel yourselves coming together. You will be CHENDELL. One being again."

We said, "These directions are confusing. Would you repeat them?"

With an exasperated eye-roll, Birú said, "You figure it out!" Then with a quickness unexpected in someone who appeared so aged, the shaman got up and went into one of the huts.

"Wait," we called as we followed Birú to the hut. But when we looked in, there was no one there. We stood in stunned silence for several minutes. It was obvious the old one wasn't coming back. We had to leave. We found our way back to the boat and began our journey back to Cocha Cashu. Back to the outside world. How would we use our new power as CHENDELL? We didn't know.

9
—

BACK TO WHAT AND HOW

Cocha Cashu Biological Station

ROBIN

We arrived just outside the station as CHENDELL. Before entering the camp, with a little trial and error, we mastered the "change" thing and appeared on the grounds as Robin and Jamie.

We asked the staff about ThreeM. They said he had been sent to a clinic in Boca Manu for treatment. His wound was healing but he had a fever and they didn't want to take any chances. He didn't say anything to anyone about the strange being who had rescued him. He was smart and undoubtedly realized that no one would believe him.

JAMIE

Fortunately, Elias and Ruben had brought back all the plant, soil and insect samples we had gathered before we encountered the illegal loggers. We made the arrangements for our departure. And at sunrise the next day, we boarded a launch for Boca Manu. From there we flew to San Francisco through Cusco and Panama.

During the long trip home, we finally had time to think and to talk. To puzzle over what had happened to us. We realized that every gift we had been given—talking with trees, directing insects—was a double-edged sword. It wasn't a game anymore. It came with responsibility. Just being able to change into CHENDELL meant we had a new purpose. How would we fulfill that purpose? We had to go back to where it all seemed to start. TransFormancy. I assured her we would figure it out.

Robin asked me, "Why do you think Birú used the number two for our changing back to our individual selves? You know. The two strokes of CHENDELL's hair."

I told her, "The number "two" has significance in China. It is considered lucky because Chinese people think all good things come in pairs. It makes sense that we stroke CHENDELL's hair two times with one eye closed and then two times with the other eye closed. We become the two of us again. A pair."

"Why do we have to use *three* hair strokes to change into CHENDELL?"

"The number three is also a lucky number," I said. "There is a similar Mandarin word that means 'life' or 'to give birth.' Isn't that what happens when we are transformed into CHENDELL? We give birth to a new life. A new life form."

Robin thought about this and then asked, "Do you think the shaman knows Mandarin?"

🍃 🍃 🍃

Mountain View, California

ROBIN

Once back in our apartment, we called Mom and Dad and Ling to tell them we were home safely. That our research trip had been successful. That it had been a life-changing experience. We didn't tell them just how life-altering it was! Then we stocked up our refrigerator with our favorite foods. Watched TV. What an act of normalcy. Catching up on the news, only to learn the world was still a mess. The next day we went into work.

JAMIE

When I saw the name on the building—TransFormancy—there was a realization that this word described what had happened to Robin and me. And I wondered why Casey Dee had chosen this name for his business. The receptionist immediately took us to Casey Dee's office. He warmly greeted us. We sat around the same coffee table we had when we first met with him. I couldn't contain myself. I asked, "What made you choose the name TransFormancy?"

Casey Dee was clearly surprised at my question. But he answered with a question of his own, "What happened in Manu?"

I parried his question. "Why did you send us there?"

He said, "I tried to discourage you. You both insisted Manu was where you wanted to go. Thousands of people have gone there and come back with no problem. That's what I hoped and wanted for you two."

I challenged him again. "What do you think happened? That we met our fate?"

"Clearly something happened to you there. You seem unsettled. I will answer any question you have but first I have to know what occurred."

"Will you believe us? Will you believe whatever we tell you?"

"I promise you I will believe you. Just tell me everything. From the beginning."

"Robin, you tell what happened."

ROBIN
I felt a sense of relief. That a great weight was going to be taken off my shoulders. Off both our shoulders. We needed to tell someone our unbelievable story. My eyes filled with tears and my throat choked up. Jamie took my hand. I composed myself and started at the beginning. Our arrival in Cusco, our trip on the river to Boca Manu, meeting up with ThreeM and on to the Cocha Cashu Research Station. Our explorations into the forest and our success at collecting samples. Our excursion up the Providencia River. Then the unexpected run-in with the illegal loggers.

At that point, as the feeling of fear came flooding back, it all became real and yet unreal at the same time. I took a minute to feel calm. Then I continued. I told him about ThreeM being shot. About Elias and Ruben disappearing. About how we ran through the forest to escape the loggers. And I told him how the forest trees saved our lives. He showed no reaction to learning of Jamie's ability to communicate with trees. But when I told him about finding the shaman, Birú, at the abandoned indigenous camp, Casey Dee's eyes filled with tears.

He said, "You and Jamie drank the old one's brew."

This part of our story was clearly familiar to him.

I replied, "Yes, we did."

"And you two were transformed into one."

"Yes."

"Go on," he said.

I told him how as one person—CHENDELL—we stopped the loggers from cutting down another mahogany tree. By using our now-combined special gifts of directing insects to fight the loggers and developing bark armor. Of fighting with kung fu techniques. Of a tree sending birds to help us. And how we saved ThreeM. I finally ended our story with trees directing us back to the shaman and what we learned. How we could change from Jamie and Robin to CHENDELL and back again. That we knew we had a purpose as CHENDELL. But we didn't know how we would fulfill this mission.

Casey Dee said, "Now I will tell you my story. I too am a transformed being. A changeling."

I said, "I am not surprised. I sensed that there was something different and yet familiar about you. But I don't like the word 'changeling.' It sounds like something out of a medieval fairytale."

Casey Dee agreed. "Of course. I do prefer 'transformed.' That's why I named my company TransFormancy. But it seems you already suspected that."

Jamie said, "I did when I saw the name on the building today. It occurred to me that 'TransFormancy' may have two meanings for you. Your transformation and your effort to transform the world."

Casey Dee continued, "I was born in India to an Indian father and mother. My name was Deepak. When I was five, my parents immigrated to England. My mother died of cancer when I was seven. My father remarried a widow. A British woman who also had a seven-year-old son. His name was Casey. My father adopted him. Casey and I became close. We were brothers. But, of course, we were different. I was the dreamer. Casey was the doer. I wanted to save everyone and everything. Casey wanted to make lots of money. We went to university. I studied animal biology. Casey studied geology.

"We went to the Peruvian rainforest—Manu National Forest—when we were both 25. I wanted to study the tamarin monkeys. Casey wanted to find minerals, especially gold. What we found was the old one, the shaman Birú. We drank the brew. We became one person. We looked like Deepak but with Casey's blue eyes and light brown hair. We made an internal agreement. He had the first 20 years to pursue his desire to make money. And then for the next 20 years, I would pursue my dream of helping mankind. After my divorce, it just made sense to use the name Casey Roy. We included the second name of Dee for Deepak.

"When it was my turn—my 20 years to have control—I used the money that Casey made to establish TransFormancy. As our environment became more and more degraded and endangered, it became apparent to me that helping people and helping the earth are intertwined goals. And one important way to improve people's lives is to ensure a healthy planet. And that means all its creatures and seas and atmosphere and foliage."

Robin inquired, "What about your wife and daughter?"

"My marriage was a casualty of our transformation. I had married young at 22 and was a father at 24. When I—we— returned looking like Deepak but acting like Casey, my wife did not accept the new person I had become. It wasn't just the blue eyes and different hair color. I made up a story about the effect of a certain rainforest plant on eye and hair color. She must have wanted to believe that silly explanation. But what she couldn't endure was the personality change. I was now a driven man. Driven to make money. I had no time for her or our child. She divorced me. In retrospect, it was a mistake to let Casey have the first 20 years. Those were years I could have had with my family."

He sighed, "Anyway I—we—immigrated to the United States where we thought we would find more opportunities. We did. We got in on the ground floor just as computers and the internet were getting started."

Jamie asked, "How many years do you have left as the good 'Casey Roy'?"

"Five more years. But we don't have any agreement for how we will live our dual life after my 20 years are over. To avoid the internal conflict we both feel about this subject, we have been avoiding it. The Casey side of us would like to spend our riches on material things. Or maybe get back into an internet business to make money.

"But the other Casey, my other half, is not a bad person. We just look at the world differently. And I must always see his viewpoint because we are a part of each other. I literally see the world through his blue eyes. We are one person with a dual mind and perspective. I use 'I' when referring to myself but it is really 'we.' We share our world through this one body."

"I'm confused," I said. "Are we are really talking to both of you?"

"Yes," he answered. "We may not always be as cohesive as we would like but the Casey part is good at directing the business side of TransFormancy. The Deepak part manages the scientific and ecological projects. We are a good team most of the time.

Clearly worried, Jamie asked, "When are you not a good team?"

Casey Dee said, "Every two people, even if they share a body, are going to have disagreements. For example, we enjoy different leisure interests. I like to read the Arts and Entertainment section of the newspaper. Casey likes to read the Business section. I like to putter in my garden. Casey likes to place stock trades. Unfortunately, even if we disagree on how to spend our time, we must be flexible and suffer through the other's activities. Didn't you two disagree when you were one?"

My answer was immediate. "No. We felt in total agreement. Our purpose as CHENDELL was clear. Though we were conscious of having one body, we thought of ourselves as 'we.' But as with you, we still had a dual awareness. And we were able to truly understand the male and female point of view."

Casey Dee laughed. "You are probably the only man and woman who can say that."

Then Casey Dee became earnest. "I want you to know something. Something important. There may be other transformed people in the world. If there are Casey and me. And you and

Jamie. Then it is possible there are others. Sometimes I speculate what would happen if two evil people were transformed into one.

"Obviously, just as the transformation of Casey and Deepak is different from the transformation of Robin and Jamie, other transformed beings could also vary. But I do think that you and Jamie are probably unique in many ways. Your combination is not just a man and a woman becoming one. It is also one being with special gifts. Communicating with trees and plants, controlling insects. Do you think you could expand your capabilities? Your control over other aspects of nature? Over animals or fish or birds?"

Jamie replied, "Robin and I have talked about the possibility of extending CHENDELL's powers. About how much the natural world might be an ally. Maybe it is possible."

Without a definitive answer to his question, Casey continued, "As CHENDELL, you have a unified purpose. And you found a way to divide and return to your former selves. That hasn't been possible for Casey and me. We have had to negotiate our dual world. Perhaps *we* need to go back to the rainforest to look for the shaman."

I sighed. "How and what do we do as CHENDELL? It feels unclear and confusing. What is the path? How do we proceed?"

Casey Dee took one of each of our hands. "You are not alone. We will figure this out together. Here at TransFormancy, you two will continue your scientific careers. You will search for the cures you want to find. We have received the shipment of specimens you both collected. They are already in your labs. But outside of this building lies CHENDELL'S mission. And I will help you fulfill your assignment."

Jamie questioned, "And that is?"

His response was, "To do what CHENDELL has done. Save the trees and the insects and all that lives and breathes. Fight those who would ruin our environment—our world—as we know it. Those people who out of greed or selfishness or foolishness kill the plants, the animals, the air, the soil, the oceans and the rivers. You will fight against ecocide. Against biocide."

Jamie said, "I have never heard that term. Biocide."

"It means the annihilation of living organisms," answered Casey Dee. "In essence, the destruction of the earth."

ROBIN
We felt inspired. Until Casey Dee continued with an unexpected question. "When you are CHENDELL, are you physically

a man or a woman? Or some sort of combination of male and female?"

JAMIE

Robin and I groaned. My quick response was, "When you see the beauty of a hawk soaring, do you wonder whether it is a male or female? If you were attacked by a ferocious tiger, would you care if it is a female or male?"

Mountain View Apartment

JAMIE

I wondered if having a dual consciousness was really that different from having a single cognizance. Don't most people always have at least two points of view or conversations with themselves? How they see themselves. How they want to be. What choices they should make. The difference for CHENDELL is that, while we maintained our dual perspectives, there was no ambiguity as to who we were. One person with one goal.

ROBIN

If we knew what lay ahead, would we have made the same choices? Or did it all happen by chance? Or was the shaman right? It was fate.

That night we sat on our sofa in our apartment and we held each other. But we did not close our eyes and stroke each other's hair three times.

Not yet.

AFTERWORD

Life's unexpected turns happen to everyone. What is essential is how we choose to view these changes. We see CHENDELL as an opportunity. A chance to make a difference. To make life better for every plant and animal on the planet Earth.

We must do our best to complete this mission—our mission. To save the world. One battle at a time.

PRONUNCIATION KEY

Bai (Bai, as in "good-bye")

Bao Wao (Bao, as in bowel), (Wao, as in "wow")

Chaoyang (district) (ciao, as we say hello "ciao"), (yang rhymes with "young")

Chen (Jinsong) (chen rhymes with "hen"), (jin, as in "gin and tonic"), (song, as in "sonar," son-)

Chunhua (chun, -un as in "raccoon"), (hua, as in schwa, hwa)

Deng (rhymes with "dung")

Dongmei (dong, as in "ding-dong"), (mei, as in "may I")

Fengtai (feng, as in "fungus"), (tai, as in "tycoon")

Gaokao (exam) (gao, as in "gown" without the n, gow-), (kao, as in "cow")

Guilin (gui, g+we as in "we are"), (lin, as in "Lynn")

Hangzhou (hang rhymes with "how") (zhou, as in "joe")

Hang Ah (restaurant) (Hang rhymes with "hung"), (ah, as in the doctor makes you say "ah")

Henan (he, as in "her") (nan, as in "naan," the bread)

Huiliang (hui, as in hu+ay, "hooray" without the r), (liang, lee+ang)

Jiang (gee+ang)

Jinsong (Chen) (jin, as in "gin and tonic"), (song, as in in "sonar," "son-"), (chen rhymes with "hen")

Jingshun (jing, as in j with ing in "king"), (shun, huuu-+ en)

Leung (Wen) (Leung, lee+ong), (wen, as in "when")

Li (River) (Li, as in "Lee")

Liang (lee+ang)

Lijuan (li, as in lee) (juan, as in drain)

Lushan Yun Wu (tea) (lu, as in "Lutheran"), (shan, as in "hey, mon!")

Ling (ling, as in "lingo")

Mei (mei, as in "May")

Mingzhu (ming, as in "Ming dynasty,"), (zhu, as in "Jew")

NianNian (nian, as in "Neanderthal")

Shanghai (shang, as in "Sean"), (hai, as in "hi-fi")

Shaolin (Kung Fu) (Shao, rhymes with "now"), (lin, as in "Lynn")

Tsinghua (University) (Tsing, as in "ching"), (hua rhymes with "hwa")

Qing (Dynasty) (qing, as in ch+ ing in "king")

Wen (Leung) (wen, as "wun" in "wunderkind" or "one of a kind")

Xian (she+yan rhymes with "she on")

Zihao (zi, as in "Nazi," -zi), (hao, as in "how") (z'how)

Zongshen (motorcycle) (zong rhymes with "zung"), (shen, as in the name "Shane")

OTHER WORDS and NAMES:

Bilial Jalbani (Bi, as in "bee"), (lal, as in "lollypop")

Amira Jalbani (Amira, as in "a miracle")

Hijab (hi, as in "he"), (jab, as in "job")

Deetjen's (Big Sur Inn) (Deet, as in "detail"), (jen, as in "Jennifer")

SPANISH WORDS and NAMES:

Acai (palm tree) (a, as in the doctor makes you say "ah"), (ca, as in "sock"), (i, as in the letter "e")

Arroz con bagre (a, as in "ah"), (rroz, as in "**roas**t" without the T), (con, as in "cone"), (ba, as in "Bob"), (gre, as in "great")

Atalaya (a, as in "ah"), (ta, as in "top"), (la, as in "lolli-pop"), (ya, y+ah)

Bacaba (tree) (ba, as in "Bob"), (ca as in "copper"), (ba, as in "Bob")

Birú (Bi, as in "bee"), (rú, as in "Rubik's cube")

Boca Manu (Bo, as in "Bo Jackson"), (ca, as in "copper"), (Ma as in "mom"), (nu as in "new")

Caimans (cai, as in "Kyle"), (manS, as in "Montreal")

Capuchins ("cappuccino" without the –ino)

Capybaras (capy rhymes with "copy"), (bara, as in "barometer")

Ceiba (tree) (cei, as in "say"), (ba, as in "Bob")

Cocha Cashu (Cocha as in "Coach a game of soccer"), (Cashu rhymes with posh-u")

Cusco (Cus, as in "couscous"), (co, as in "co-pay")

Ipê (tree) (i-pé, like "eBay," but ePay)

Jaguar (pronounced like ha – gwar)

Manu (National Park) (Ma, as in "mom"), (nu, as in "new")

Manuel Mendez Montero (Man, as in "Montreal"), (uel rhymes with "well"), (Men, as in "a few good men"), (dez rhymes with "says"), (Mon rhymes with "cone") (tero rhymes with "marrow")

Mashco Piro (Mash rhymes with "posh"), (co, as in "co-pay"), (Pi, as in "peek"), (ro, as in "roux," rhymes with "new")

Matsigenka (machigengue) (ma-chee-gain-gay) Can be pronounced two ways. (ma, as in "macho"), (chee, as in "cheese"), (gain), (gay, as in "gay") or (ma, as in "macho"), (tsi, as in "nazi"), (gain), (gay, as in "gay")

Maya (Ma, as in "Montreal"), (ya, as in y+ah)

Providencia (River) (Pro, as in "pro" athlete), (vi, as in "veer" to the left), (den, as in "dense"), (ia, as in "Mama Mia")

Senor (señor)

Senora (señora)

Tamarin (ta, as in "Tom"), (ma, as in "Mom"), (rin rhymes with "gin")

Yine (Yi, as in "yee haw"), (ne, as in "yay or nay")

ACKNOWLEDGMENTS

In making the story of CHENDELL a reality, I learned that writing a book is only part of the process. The other part is the involvement, support and aid of those who have enhanced my vision and made the experience richer.

First and foremost, I thank my husband, Martin, for believing in my book 100% and in me 200%. CHENDELL exists because of his support, advice and assistance.

A special thank you to Armella Stepan, who went beyond the call of duty with her caring nature, indefatigable support and professional guidance.

Thank you to Michael J. Jackson for his invaluable help of mentoring me and connecting me to Armella Stepan.

I am especially grateful to Susan Agrest for her enthusiasm, praise and continuous proofreading. She kept me going.

To the insightful coaches and veteran writers, my appreciation and thanks to Judy Babb for her exceptional editing skills and to Jim Hull for challenging me to envision CHENDELL's future.

Many thanks to the talented and flexible Naomi Alessandra Shultz for her visionary art.

My deep appreciation to Bob Sommer and Brandon Stout of Changing Hands Bookstore for their helpful suggestions and valuable information.

I want to thank the following for their generous contributions: Thom Racina, Ivor Davis, Kathy Roth, Hessa Al-Saraj and my brother, Larry Krause, for their encouragement; Paula Kuespert, Neil Butwin and my niece, Danielle Simon, for their assistance; Krishna Curry for expanding my cultural awareness; Diane Namm for starting me on this journey; and Jeff Erhart for his invaluable feedback.

And finally, thank you to the Beijing and Guilin communities who helped make my trip to China a memorable and wonderful experience. I found the good heart of Chen Jinsong in the kindness of the Chinese people.

ABOUT LESLIE I. LANDIS

Leslie Landis (www.chendell.com) is the author of *CHENDELL: A Natural Warrior*. She holds a master's degree in psychology. Her broad experience includes working for a U.S. Senator and as an associate director in television. Leslie lives in Los Angeles with her husband. They are momentarily adopting 2 dogs.

Made in the USA
Coppell, TX
20 February 2020